Para una
Buena Secretaria
Juan

Enjoy

Dog: An Immigrant Story

By Pete Buczkowski

Authored with Lynda Durrant

Cover illustration by Diana Durrant

Dog by Lynda Durrant

WWII, Poland, Venezuela, Immigrants to the United States of America, Thomas Jefferson, the pursuit of happiness, Space Age

YA and Adult fiction

ISBN-13:978-1539177425
ISBN-10:1539177424

Green Heron Press

Chapter One
The Cold

Hola, amigos! This is a story about Dog.

Dog is a rooster. Papa says he is an araucana *gallo*, the native South American rooster. Mama calls his feathers iridescent—as though Dog's feathers are shimmering with electricity. His breast and tail feathers are golden yellow. His wings and back are jungle green. Brilliant red feathers line his throat. His leg feathers are the same color as the shiny brownish-yellow plantains, the native bananas that hang in bunches from the tall trees around our village. His razor-sharp claws are as sparkling black as the starry night sky.

Why is my fearless rooster named Dog, and how did he come to live with a Polish family named Buczkowski in Venezuela? Why is his fierce courage our best hope in this, our brand new future? *Amigos*, I am already getting ahead of the story. I must go back to the very, very beginning. I must begin with the cold.

As Papa likes to say, the war is over and those Nazis no longer call the tune. Those German pigs (*Niemskie swinie* in Polish) have been thrashed, defeated totally, and in the dustbin of history. It's been twelve years since World War II ended. The world is well rid of them and free once more.

I'm not so sure.

By day, Mama hoards food because she's sure we'll all die of starvation by the end of next week. We're poor, but never hungry.

By night, Mama screams out loud her nightmares. Each time, my brothers and I leap from our bed in terror. As my mother screams, I imagine those Nazi *swinie* grunting, wallowing in the mud, and smirking at the Buczkowskis. Papa holds Mama until she falls asleep again. I hold my whimpering brothers until they fall asleep again. Three hours later Mama is screaming once more about the cold, the rats, and the potatoes.

In September 1939, Hitler's German army invaded Poland. Papa likes to quote the Emperor Napoléon Bonaparte: "An army marches on its stomach." The German army needed potatoes and winter was only months away. My parents were potato slaves in Hitler's work camps.

Mama was sent to a slave camp first. She was only 13. From sun up to sundown she worked in the potato fields to grow food for Hitler's army. Mama's parents, her brothers and sisters, aunts and uncles, her cousins? She never saw any of them again.

In 1940, Papa was sent to the same slave camp. He was 18. There my parents met, in the potato fields. Hitler's slaves grew potatoes, but weren't allowed to eat any. When my parents were slaves to the Nazis, they lived on water, rats, and raw, stolen potatoes.

My father never saw anyone in his family again, either.

My parents remember war-time Polish winters so cold slaves froze to death in their sleep. They say the dead's thin blankets were given to the living in the hope that they would live to see another sun rise.

In the freezing dawn, my parents would march out into the potato fields. They'd plow through the snow drifts and dig into the frozen ground with their bare hands. They hoped they'd find enough potatoes to fill their daily regulation basket, and maybe a frozen spud or two to fill their own stomachs.

Mama has said I have her youngest brother's eyes—the same pale gray as the pearly light just before dawn. My father has told me I have his father's square jaw. Both say I have their mothers' smiles. When I was little, I squinted into the mirror and pretended my dead relatives were looking back at me.

Now that I am twelve, I see only myself.

When the war ended in 1945, my parents moved to a Displaced Persons camp in West Germany, a DP camp. I was born there, in 1947. Papa applied for visas to any nation taking refugees—The United States, The United Kingdom, Canada, Australia, New Zealand, South Africa, Venezuela, Argentina, and Brazil.

Papa's first choice was the United States, but Venezuela chose us. Papa paddled us by dugout canoe to our village. Welcome to the stunning heat and humidity of Venezuela.

We live in a Quonset hut, abandoned by the *Norte Americanos* after one of their petroleum companies laid a pipeline for oil from our village to the Caribbean Sea. The oil men left ten huts: our section of the village. The Quonset huts are curved sheets of hammered metal, like half a hollow log cut lengthwise and laid on the ground.

The name of our village is New Barcelona, named after the city in Spain. We live on the Orinoco River, and so deep in the Amazon jungle we don't see the sun for days on end.

Our section is a closed circle of ten Quonset huts for the DP families, the mayor's house, our school, and the barber shop. The rest of our village is made up of Venezuelans, but they live outside our circle. Except for the mayor, we don't talk to them.

The cold.

I don't know what it means to be cold. Papa says before the war, cold was fleeting, so in that sense it was fun. The cold weather always meant coming inside to become warm and cozy again. It meant hot chocolate and turning your toes toward the crackling hearth fire.

Once, when Papa was a child, he turned his toes so close to the hearth his socks caught fire. As he hopped up and down in the kitchen, his brothers and sisters laughed so hard hot chocolate sprayed from their nostrils. His mother heard his screams and threw him out in the snow to douse the flames.

Mama said when she was a child, her mother used to look out the kitchen window for signs of the spring, for a change in the weather.

I don't understand what a change in the weather means. I've never known a day that wasn't steaming hot.

The jungle never stops sneaking up on us. Every morning, the men and boys take our machetes in hand to cut it back. Every night the jungle creeps closer. Some mornings we have a little extra time to cut the jungle back a bit further. The next morning, there is less jungle to chop.

Is this like a change in the weather? Is this what it means to be cold?

Papa says I should think about the loneliest and saddest I have ever felt, plus exhausted, hungry, forsaken, and hopeless. He said to think about feeling this way for years with no hope of becoming warm and safe again. Cold is not fleeting, and not soothed by hot chocolate. Cold kills by the millions. Cold means no hope.

When I was five, my parents and I were in the mayor's house for his annual Christmas party. Mama gave me a chip of ice from his wife's electric refrigerator-freezer.

"Pedrito, this is what cold feels like," she said as she held it to my cheek.

The ice felt like fire as it slowly turned to water and dripped down my chin. "Imagine that feeling all over—your arms, legs, neck, and chest. Imagine your toes and fingers as cold and stiff as that ice chip. That is cold. That's why I never, ever want to be cold again."

I've tried to picture it. The mayor's massive refrigerator-freezer is a Coldspot, from Milwaukee, Wisconsin. It purrs like a well-fed jungle cat. I've tried pretending, to be stuck in an ice chip, or bobbing like a cork in a cold spot, but I can't imagine such icy terror. This is the stuff of Mama's nightmares.

I don't want to feel such frozen despair. And, where was God in all this? Why did He abandon my parents and millions of others just like them? I want everyone to be happy, happy in his or her own way.

That's why I'm ready to tell about Dog.

Chapter Two

The Egg

It's an early Saturday morning in December, and Mama shines a candle in my face. Before I can say anything, she is shushing. "Don't wake your father, Pedrito. This is his only morning to sleep in. Why are the chickens so noisy?"

I dress, grab the candlestick, and my machete. Why are the chickens squawking? The jungle teems with arrow snakes, rattlesnakes, 500-pound green anacondas, boa constrictors, scorpions, boars, jaguars, monkeys, alligators—lots of animals would like an egg for breakfast.

Mama used to collect our eggs but one morning a bird spider on the chicken coop wall sent her running back to her kitchen. Now it's my job to collect the eggs.

Why are the chickens clucking their heads off?

Our chicken coop is around the back by our shower and toilet stalls. I open the wooden door with my foot. The candlelight shines into every corner, every nest. What am I looking for? Snakeskin or the stark black of a bird spider (the size of a man's hand) on the whitewashed walls.

The candle is in my left hand. My machete is in my right. No predators, but there's something very wrong, for the *gallinas,* the hens, are jumping from their nests and flapping their wings in my face. "Be quiet," I shout before I forget that Papa is sleeping. I say softly, "There're no egg thieves this morning. Be quiet."

One *gallina* flaps straight up from her nest, higher than the rest. Her chicken eyes are bugged out in fear and alarm.

I shine the candle into her nest. What I see makes me almost drop it into the straw. For there in her nest is a gigantic egg! The biggest I have ever seen in all the time I have gathered eggs for Mama. The egg is sky blue with brown spots--the same rich brown of our Christmas chocolate bars from Hershey, Pennsylvania.

Never have I seen such colors on a hen's egg before.

Now the *gallina* is squawking around my feet as if to say, "Pedrito! I did not lay that egg! It's not from me! I did not lay that monstrosity! Get it out of my nest before anyone else sees it."

I take it outside for a better look. As soon as the egg is out of the coop, the chickens quiet down.

In that moment of silence the sun breaks over the horizon.

An instant later, the roosters of Venezuela are waking up and announcing the day. The jungle birds chime in. Squawks, calls, cockles, caws, and delicate singing wake everyone, both people and animals, including Papa.

What about the egg? I'll say nothing, for didn't the *gallina* ask me to take it away and not tell anyone it was hers? I roll it under the Venus fly trap bush near our front door. I dash back into the coop and gather seven eggs.

"What was the ruckus?" Mama asks me as I sit down to breakfast.

I give her an elaborate shrug. "Who knows? Chickens worry too much."

Papa laughs. "Chickens are too stupid to worry. Only those who have the wisdom to know about tomorrow know enough to worry."

Mama mutters, "Lucky chickens." It is Mama's job to fetch our daily water from the spigot in the center of our village. She ladles the eggs into a pot of boiling water. "Wash your hands, Pedrito."

When I return, Mama ladles streaming rice into our rice bowls. She cracks soft-boiled eggs onto the rice—two each for Mama and Papa, one each for me and my two little brothers. Myron is seven; Zenon is three.

As always, we wait while Papa gives thanks. He gives thanks to God for the miracle of food, for when my parents were teenagers there was no food. To my parents, breakfast, lunch, and dinner are daily miracles.

Myron speaks up. "Is today Food Feast day, Papa?"

"Yes," Papa returns. He smiles at Mama, who nods to him.

It is part of the morning routine—my parents look up from their rice and eggs and smile at each other. They clink their juice glasses together. The pink guava juice—thick with pulp—trembles in their glasses.

"To our survival," Papa says. He tosses his head back and drinks his guava juice in one big gulp.

"To our liberation." Mama sips hers but finishes it before setting the glass down on the table again.

"To Food Feast day," Myron shouts.

"To Food Feast day," Papa says, his voice choking with thankfulness.

The kerosene lamp hanging above our table sings. I salt and pepper my egg. In the wavering light, the white and black specks glow on the yolk, as deep orange as a Venezuelan sunrise.

On Saturdays, my parents go to the city marketplace in Puerto La Cruz to buy staples and perishable food, especially meat. Saturday is the only day in the week we have meat for dinner. Unlike the mayor's wife, we do not have a Coldspot refrigerator-freezer.

My father leases land from the mayor. Papa grows the best tomatoes, fiery hot chili peppers, sweet peppers, and yellow onions.

He tried to explain once about a growing season. "In Poland," he said, "seeds are planted in May and the vegetables are harvested from July through October. Food doesn't grow in the winter. It's too cold."

I wanted to ask what people eat in the winter but his eyes watered. To my parents, cold will be linked forever to loss, grief, and starvation. But there in their frigid pasts are the clues to understanding them, just like peeling back the layers of one of Papa's yellow onions.

My brothers and I load Papa's vegetables into Señor Nicholas's oxen cart. We three walk behind it to the neighboring village's market. The road to the marketplace is blood-red dust.

The jungle crouches toward the road, ready to pounce. Our mayor says there wasn't a road between the villages when he was a boy. He remembers packing vegetables in a straw basket and strapping it onto his back. He had to walk through the grasping jungle to bring his family's produce to market.

After a half an hour later, three-year-old Zenon starts to whimper. This is his signal—I pick him up and carry him the rest of the way.

It is my job to sell the vegetables. It is Myron's job to use Mama's broom to chase away the flies, bees, spiders, birds, and monkeys that would like to sample Papa's produce. It is Zenon's job to thank our customers.

The marketplace is busy today. Yanomani tribesmen, Venezuelans, and European refugees crowd the stands. Venezuelans call us Europeans *Blancos.*

By late afternoon, all my father's vegetables are sold. It's time to go home. Señor Nicholas always buys my brothers and me shave-ice cones. Myron likes guava and shares his with Zenon. I prefer mango. My brothers and I get to sit in Señor Nicholas's oxen cart on the way back to New Barcelona.

As the cart shudders into the potholes, I think about my egg. Is it still there? Have the village rats taken it away? Has a jaguar or capybara dragged it from under the Venus fly trap bush for a quick meal?

As always, Zenon falls asleep against my shoulder, his face sticky and stained pink from shave ice. I lick the hem of my shirt and wipe his mouth. The sun is beginning to set when Señor Nicolas pulls into the New Barcelona village common. Myron runs inside our hut. Zenon toddles after him.

"Food Feast!" Myron shouts.

Before I go inside, I steal a quick look at my egg. Within her largest mouth, the Venus fly trap has caught something brown and buzzing; its antennas wriggle still.

My egg lies underneath, as still as a rock.

Chapter Three

Hits the Spot

Our hut fills with the savory scents of Saturday night dinner. Venezuelans love meat, especially beef. Mama has simmered shredded beef and chicken in spicy gravy. She serves it with rice, black beans, and pancakes made of fresh corn called *cachapas.*

My mouth waters as I sit down to our table.

Before the Food Feast begins, Papa looks at me with lifted eyebrows. Proudly, I give him the coins we earned today selling his vegetables. Mama watches closely as the coins tumble from my palm onto the table.

"Pedrito," Mama says, "wash your hands. You don't know where those coins have been."

As I wash my hands, my mouth waters more. Mama's *bischoho*—her beef and chicken stew—is my favorite.

Mama serves up her *bischoho* and there's plenty left for seconds. For dessert we have fried bread sprinkled with sugar. My brothers and I always share a Pepsi-Cola, bottled in Miami, Florida. The Pepsi is still cool from the Puerto La Cruz marketplace.

All through the Saturday Food Feast we ask one another questions:

"In what country do people eat beef and chicken every day?"

"America!"

"In what country do people have cars, sometimes two per family?"

"America!"

"In what country do children go to school in buildings as big as our village?"

"America!"

"In what country do people have electric refrigerators and stoves, and a special machine that washes dishes?" Mama always asks this one.

"America!"

"In what country do people have both a job and a garden? They have both money and food?" Papa always asks this one.

"America!"

I try to imagine such a country, where electric machines do all the work, where schools are the size of

New Barcelona, where people live on beef, chicken, and chocolate bars, and drink Pepsi-Cola every day. It seems as mysterious and remote as a Polish winter.

People are shouting. "Our visas! Our visas have arrived!"

Papa looks up from his *bischoho.* "Somebody is going to America."

We bolt from our table and hurry outside. It's the Zalenskys—all five of them race around the soccer field in the village common, whooping and hollering. Mrs. Zalensky stops, kneels in the dirt, and begins to sob.

"Where are you going?" Papa calls out.

"Walla Walla, Washington," Mr. Zalensky returns. "On Monday, we're going to America. America!" he shouts.

Myron and I look at one another. "Walla Walla, Washington?" I mutter.

Myron shrugs. "Maybe George's papa was named Walla Walla."

"Maybe."

My friend Tomas Zalensky is thirteen and a great soccer player. I hope Walla Walla, Washington appreciates his wicked skill as a midfield striker.

Mama sighs. "When will our visas arrive? When will our lives begin?"

"Let's go in, boys," Papa says. "Our dinners are getting cold. We'll get our visas soon." Papa holds Mama's hand. "My cousin in Cleveland has promised to sponsor us. Soon, you'll see."

How can I persuade Mama to welcome my egg into the family?

"I have to check the horses' blankets." This is the sentence we use to go outside to use the toilet.

"Come right back, Pedrito," Mama says. "It's your turn to wash the dishes."

As I shut the front door, Myron asks, "In what country do people have a toilet inside the house?"

Zenon giggles. "Stinky!"

The sun set an hour ago. In total darkness, I feel under the Venus flytrap. I pull out my egg and hold it with both hands.

Mama has strict food rules. Eggs are for breakfast seven mornings a week, and for Christmas and Easter cakes. When a hen is too old to lay eggs she's killed, and then boiled for hours to tenderize her for a Saturday Food Feast. The next Saturday, Papa returns from the Puerto La Cruz marketplace with a young laying chicken.

Mama has said, again and again, the Buczkowskis do not keep pets. Animals are food.

Mama is standing next to the dry sink. She's washing the dishes for me. Later, I'll walk onto one of the jungle paths and throw out the soapy water. Mama is too frightened of the jungle to take even one step into it.

"Look what I have." I stand in the center of our hut. Slowly, I uncurl my hands to reveal the egg.

"Breakfast!" my father shouts. "Look at the size of it! I'll need only one egg for breakfast tomorrow."

"Papa, I can take care of this egg. I can hatch it. It will be mine to care for and feed."

"No pets," my mother says flatly as she turns from the sink. "You know the rules, Pedrito. We don't have enough food to feed the five of us."

My heart sinks. Mama will never lose her obsession with food. Never. For her, starvation will always lurk in a dark corner, grinning and beckoning to her as a skin-and-bones ghost.

Those Nazis, those *Niemskie swinie,* are still calling the tune, still wallowing in the mud, still smirking at the Buczkowskis.

"I can take care of this egg. I can hatch it. I know I can."

"That egg will serve as your father's Sunday breakfast, the man who puts food on this table, young man."

"But Mama, this egg is big. That means the chicken inside will be big. It can guard the rest of the chickens." Myron and Zenon stand in front of me and stare, wide-eyed, at the egg.

Mama throws her dishrag on the counter. "What if it eats the rest of the chickens? You don't know what it means, to be surrounded by people who have starved to death."

"It won't eat the chickens. There's corn—"

"Not from my kitchen. You don't know what it means to be starving to death, to not care if you live or die."

Papa holds his right hand up. This is a signal for everyone else to stop talking. A long moment of silence stretches out….

"What could come out of an egg that size?" Papa asks softly. "There could be anything in there. Pedrito should take on the responsibility. He's old enough."

"How do you know it's fertilized?" Mama snaps.

"Let's candle it."

Papa holds the egg three inches from the kerosene lantern. I squint hard but I don't see anything. Myron squints, too. Zenon jumps up as he tries to see.

Papa says, "I see a beak and two claws. It's fertilized, probably laid about a week ago. Wild roosters live in the jungle. Brilliant feathers." Papa shakes his head in wonder. "There could be anything in there."

"I want to take care of whatever is in there, to prove that the future will be better than the past, better…than the present."

Papa turns to me. "Pedrito, there's an old Pepsi-Cola box by the chicken coop. Fill it with straw and bring it in. You'll need to keep the egg warm."

Myron and I run out the back door.

That evening, my egg is wrapped in one of Mama's dish towels and nestled in straw. On the box, the words Pepsi-Cola Hits the Spot flicker and dance in the candlelight.

"Now what?" Zenon whispers. My brothers and I all sleep in the same bed.

"Now we wait."

I blow out the candle and drop off to sleep. I dream about my egg's father. A wild rooster struts the jungle paths as he waits for his son to be born.

Chapter Four

Opulencia

It is the next Friday afternoon after school.

I stand on our side of the Zimmer family's bridge. "*Hola,* Anatole," I shout. "Tolic, can you hear me?"

The Orinoco River winds slowly just below my feet. On its sunny banks caimans bask; that's the South American alligator. Most have long since been eaten. The wily few that remain are huge and stare at me with blank, unreadable eyes. Are they thinking of eating me?

I shout again across the bridge, "*Hola,* Anatole Zimmer. Tolic!"

My friend Anatole—Tolic for short—leans out of his bedroom window. His eyeglasses catch the late afternoon light as white disks. I'm not sure he sees me, but then he waves and beckons. "Pedrito," he calls out.

Only then do I cross the Zimmer's bridge.

The Zimmers live in the biggest house in New Barcelona; not even the mayor lives in a house this size. It was built to look like a mansion in the most fashionable part of Berlin: brick with tall, white-trimmed windows; a semi-circular drive; and a pitched roof of shining, hammered copper. It has *hacienda* touches as well, as is proper for the Venezuelan house of a rich man: a fountain bubbles in the front yard; a terra cotta terrace flanks one side of the house; and a swimming pool and tennis court flank the other.

Tolic's father has a putting green behind the house.

Tolic's parents fled Germany in the spring of 1939—just six months before Hitler invaded Poland and the war began. They were able to take their money, their automobile, their art, and their furniture with them. Once the war started, those fleeing Nazi Germany had to leave everything behind so Hitler could seize it to pay for his war.

At the Zimmer's house, native Venezuelans are a constant, swarming army of tutors, gardeners, maids, cooks, and chauffeurs. Tolic told me there is a *Manito*—a young man—with a net who arrives each dawn to scoop snakes and alligators out of the swimming pool. Every six weeks, the roofers return to scrub the *verdete* spores—the greenish-grey verdigris—from the brilliant copper roof.

"Pedrito, come into the kitchen for some hot chocolate."

"*Gracias, amigo.*"

In the kitchen, Tolic asks for hot chocolate for two. Their cook nods, and drops everything to prepare it.

We sit in the cool shade of the back porch. The sweet jungle air, heavy with humidity, floats as a pale rainbow above Herr Zimmer's putting green. Tolic's mother cultivates orchids. Pink, purple, magenta, yellow, and white orchids spill out like waterfalls from between the broad leaves. Bougainvillea, hibiscus, and bird-of-paradise thrive in washtub-size Chinese porcelain pots.

The cook serves our hot chocolate in delicate china cups and saucers, with a plate of cookies on the side. She leaves the silver tray on the table.

"*Muchas Gracias*," I say to her.

The hot chocolate is sweet and spicy, for the Venezuelans drink it with cinnamon and a touch of cayenne pepper. It's just the right temperature—not too hot—for sipping right now. I feel the cayenne pepper's tickle in the back of my throat. I reach for a cookie.

I have sat in the Zimmer's kitchen and watched their cook make these cookies. They are both crisp and crumbly, made with butter, ground Brazil nuts, and Mexican vanilla. The cook molds the cookies into half-moon shapes, and dredges them in powdered sugar just after baking them. She calls them *la Galletas de ángel*—angel cookies.

Opulencia, I think. Such opulence I can't even dream of.

"Tolic, come and see my egg. It's huge. My parents are letting me keep it, to let it hatch. The shell is sky blue with chocolate- brown flecks."

Tolic grins. "An enormous egg?" he asks in English. "Maybe a triceratops will hatch out of it."

I laugh and reply in English. "Not so enormous."

Tolic has a copy of *The Enormous Egg*; by Oliver Butterworth, published by Little, Brown and Company in Boston, Massachusetts. Tolic helped me read it, because Papa and Mama want me to learn English. Someday, I'll read *The Enormous Egg* to my little brothers.

We switch back to Spanish. "Come see my egg, Tolic. You won't believe how big it is."

"I have to tell my parents where I'm going."

Tolic jumps to his feet and runs upstairs. He's

left half of his hot chocolate it in his cup and two angel cookies on his plate.

Quickly, I gobble down the cookies and drink the rest of his hot chocolate.

Tolic returns. He doesn't notice that his snack is gone.

We cross the Zimmer's bridge into the Displaced Persons side, the DP side, of New Barcelona. The Venezuelans call us Delayed Pilgrims because it's no secret our parents dream of going to the United States someday. Mama dreams of Key West, Florida, where she'll never be cold again. Papa dreams of Pasadena, California, because he wants his sons to work for the Jet Propulsion Lab. He wants us to become rocket scientists.

"I'm home," I announce to my parents. "I want to show Tolic my egg."

My parents are at our table, reading newspapers under our kerosene lamp. They sit under a halo of singing yellow light. Zenon is playing by himself in the corner.

Papa's face lights up. "Anatole, *guten tag*," he says. "This 'good day' is his signal to Tolic that he'd like to practice his German.

Tolic's face lights up, too. "*Guten tag*, Herr Buczkowski." He is too polite to ask my father to call him by his nickname.

For a few minutes, Papa and Tolic chat in German. I know enough German to follow but not enough to join in. Papa asks about his parents. Tolic tells Papa they are going to Rio de Janeiro, Brazil, for the Christmas holidays.

Papa asks Tolic to take photographs of the American airplane, the Douglas DC-7, made by the Douglas Aircraft Company in Long Beach, California.

I regard my father with pride but my heart breaks. He has told me, again and again, that to be multi-lingual is a European's birthright. Here he is chatting in German, with Cuban, French-Canadian, and Venezuelan newspapers at his fingertips. He could be in a café in Bonn, Paris, London, Madrid, or Amsterdam.

But those fingertips are stained dark red from the Venezuelan soil he tills. His farmer's pants and work shirt are ragged hand-me-downs from a Methodist church mission in Oklahoma City, Oklahoma. His neck and face are sunburned. His battered farmer's boots are tied together with binder's twine.

Tolic promises to take photographs of the Douglas DC-7. He has his father's Zeiss Ikon, a German camera made before the war.

As they chat, Mama's face becomes darker and darker. She stands up abruptly, muttering about rich Nazis under her breath.

Papa gasps at her in horror. "Uncivilized! Rude!" he shouts.

Mama runs to the front door but won't go outside, for the jungle terrifies her. She runs to the back door, stops once more. Finally, she stands in front of our sink and turns her back.

Quickly, I drag the Pepsi-Cola box forward. I unwrap my egg.

"Pedrito, when was it laid?" Tolic asks as he peers at it.

I steal a glance at Tolic. His eyes and cheeks burn bright—so he does know the Polish term for rich Nazis—*bogate Nazisci.*

"It was laid more than ten days ago."

Papa won't switch to Polish. His German is clear and firm. "It might be an araucana."

Tolic exclaims in German, "An araucana! They were brought to Chile by Chinese explorers, centuries before Columbus."

"Only half araucana," I say in Spanish, for my egg's mother is a plain white hen. Mama stands in front of our sink, her face to the wall. Our Quonset hut has only the two windows, but even in the dimness, I see her shoulders and neck trembling in anger and outrage.

"Wild roosters live in the jungle," Papa says. "There could be anything in there."

Tolic looks at his Swiss watch. He switches back to Spanish. "It's time for me to go home. I'd like to see what hatches from your egg."

"I'll walk you to your bridge."

Tolic is still blushing. He's staring at the floor.

"*Lebewohl,* Anatole," Papa says. His 'goodbye' is certainly loud enough for Mama to hear. She is only three feet away from us.

"*Guten tag,* Herr Buczkowski," Tolic replies.

He bows toward my mother's back. "Señora Buczkowski."

Mama doesn't reply.

The late afternoon sun presses down on our heads like a fat schoolbook. We walk to the Zimmer's bridge, scuffing our shoes against the red dust. My shoes are Oklahoma City hand-me-downs. His are sturdy Buster Brown's—made in Clayton, Missouri—and brand new.

Tolic's eyeglasses have slid down his sweating nose. He pushes them back into place. "My father was not a Nazi."

"I know that."

"He owned an eyeglass factory in Berlin."

"Mama lost everyone in her family. She hates Germans."

Tolic kicks up a large puff of red dust. It hovers in the sultry air before slowly sinking. "I know that," he says sadly.

He hesitates, and then speaks softly. "Papa is a Jehovah's Witness."

"What's that?"

"Not a Nazi."

"Oh. Listen. Stefan, Ivan, and I are fishing for alligators next Sunday. I've got two lizard legs out in the jungle. You won't believe the stink."

His face brightens immediately. "We won't be leaving for Rio de Janeiro until the next day. I'll be there with some bait, too"

Mama is preparing dinner when I return: rice, and vegetables from Papa's garden. Our floor is packed dirt. Our beds are Venezuelan army surplus cots. Our kitchen chairs and table are hammered together slats from packing crates. Our pillows and blankets are threadbare Oklahoma City hand-me-downs.

As Mama cooks, she bangs her battered pots and pans against the two-ring gas stove. Vegetables fly in the air as she chops.

The heat is stifling--I want a cool Pepsi-Cola, but Food Feast is tomorrow night. Papa has said we might get Hershey bars for Christmas. We might. My brother Myron holds a fierce love for chocolate.

Papa watches me closely. “You’ve been to Anatole’s house?”

“We had angel cookies and hot chocolate.”

“Ah.”

My eyes flood with tears. “Why are we so poor, Papa?” I whisper. “Why does his family have so much? Why do we have so little?”

“Anatole’s a good friend. Life is unjust. Keep the two separate.”

Mama throws chopped vegetables into her saucepan. They sizzle angrily.

Chapter Five
This is For You

We Displaced Persons are from Russia, and Poland, the Ukraine, and Belarus. All these countries were invaded and occupied by the Nazis. The Poles, the Ukrainians, the Russians, and the Belarusians all speak similar languages, like cousins in the same family tree.

We DP kids speak Spanish in school and on the soccer field. At home, anything goes. I speak Spanish to my brothers. My parents speak to us in Polish.

There are a few DPs from Germany and Italy. In World War II, the Germans, Italians, and Japanese fought together against the rest of the world.

As Papa likes to say, those Nazis no longer call the tune. Those *Niemskie swinie* no longer control events. Our side didn't start the war and we're the victors. Why would the winners hold a grudge? Let's put the past behind us.

I'm not so sure.

The German and Italian men among us now say they were in the Underground. They tell elaborate stories of working in secret to defeat Hitler's Nazis and Mussolini's fascists. They declare themselves as Allies, and winners, too. Papa says we should let them believe we believe them.

It is the DP women who hold onto their bitterness with both fists.

Mama flatly refuses to treat the German and Italian DPs with kindness and courtesy. She says to treat them as a good neighbor is a betrayal to her family, who died at the hands of the Nazis. She will never forget. Never.

Mama says the Italians are just as bad because their leader, Benito Mussolini, was a partner with Hitler. She will never forgive. Never.

If she ever meets a Japanese she'd say the same thing. Never forgive. Never forget.

"This is for you!"

"This is for you!"

The Señorías Rusanowsky and Napoli are fighting over the poodle dress again. The DPs depend on clothing from church missions in Oklahoma City, from Elkhart, Indiana, from Amarillo, Texas, from Naples, Florida, from Columbia, Missouri, from all over.

Last June, a large box from the Amarillo Baptists had caught the eye of every Señoría with daughters, for it was packed solid with dresses, skirts, girls' blouses, anklets, and girls' shoes. Mama had no interest, but the women with daughters fought so hard over that box, the mayor had to fire his pistol in the air to restore order. But order was not restored.

Señoría Napoli and Señoría Rusanowsky had both seized a pink dress with a black poodle family at the hemline. Each wanted it for her daughter and would not let go. The mayor decided the girls should share the dress.

It was Señoría Rusanowsky who started the mooning. She accused Señoría Napoli of hoarding the dress. Señoría Napoli tossed her head; she claimed her daughter wasn't ready to wear it yet. There was no occasion special enough, here in New Barcelona. Señoría Rusanowsky and her daughter would just have to wait.

Señoría Rusanowsky's face turned tabasco pepper red. She turned her back, pulled up her dress, and pulled down her underwear. "*Italyanskya,* this is for you!" she screamed. Her bare ass is as pale as the palest-pink orchid petals.

Señoría Napoli screamed, "*Russa*, this is for you!" Señoría Napoli turned her back, pulled up her dress, and pulled down her underwear. Her ass is the same dull white of alligator eggs. As she shakes it, it wobbles.

Whenever the men and boys of New Barcelona hear, "This is for you!" we all come running, even Tolic has run across his family's bridge fast enough to catch a good look. Señores Rusanowsky and Napoli come running the fastest, to order their wives to behave themselves.

It was two years ago last September when the Orinoco River overflowed.

A German family named Mueller used to live on the riverbank. We all watched in horror as the roaring Orinoco lifted their Quonset hut as though it were an umbrella and tumbled it downstream toward the Caribbean Sea.

Our men raced after the Mueller's hut.

Darkness fell. The DP mothers wouldn't give the Mueller family a place to stay for the night. Each turned her back.

Señoría Mueller sank to her knees and wept bitterly. As Señor Mueller shushed her, she claimed to have always hated Hitler. Always.

"Let them suffer," Mama whispered bitterly. "It's the least they deserve."

That evening, the Muellers slept in the village common with the clothes on their backs. At dawn, the five muddy Muellers held hands and walked together into the jungle. Within seconds, the thick green wall knitted up behind them, with nothing but swaying leaves to show they'd been there.

That evening, our men returned empty-handed. No one told them about the Muellers. No one said one word. Our men didn't ask, either.

The Muellers walked into the jungle between Stefan Bliatok's house and the mayor's house. For a long time afterward, I'd stop on my way to school, or to Stefan's house, or to the soccer field, and look closely at that spot.

Our teacher, Señor Gutiérrez, put me into the geometry class with the older students last spring. Our school has one compass and two protractors and we're all supposed to share. Of course, the teenagers won't share with me because I'm twelve. Papa had taught me how to make my own compass with a piece of string tied to a pencil, and my thumb pressing down on the other end of the string.

"There," he'd said as he drew on our table, "a perfect circle. Now you can measure the angles and add and subtract them."

"Thank you, Papa."

He sighed as his shoulders caved in. "I worry about you, Pedrito. You have a gift, a golden head for math. How will you use your gift here in the jungle? We have to go to America."

Anyway, our teacher taught us that a circle is strongest when it's closed. It's simple geometry. Maybe the Muellers will come back, walk into our closed circle of DPs once more and we'd all pretend nothing had happened. As Papa said, we should let them believe we believe them.

The Yanomani tribesmen are cannibals—that's what our mayor has told us. Also, the Amazon River basin is bursting with poisonous snakes, lizards, spiders, and tree frogs.

Maybe the Muellers will return, close the circle, but they walked into the jungle because they had no other place to go. And it's been two years. They haven't come back.

Chapter Six
Gater Taters

Early Sunday morning, Tolic knocks politely at our front door. He's dressed as though he's going on an African safari, with khaki pants, a matching shirt and multi-pocketed vest, and a wide-brimmed pith helmet covered in mosquito netting. Around his shoulders is an expensive leather-and-canvas fishing creel.

He's brought his magnifying glass with him, for inspecting my egg. I drag the Pepsi-Cola box to our open front door for the better light.

Gently, I unroll the egg from Mama's dishtowel.

"Are you sure it's fertilized?" Tolic asks. His bright blue eye behind the magnifying glass is huge and inquisitive.

"Papa grew up on a farm. He candled the shell and saw claws and a beak. The box is in the sunlight all day. At night, I've been sleeping with the egg under my chin. It should hatch any day now. Would you like some breakfast?"

My enormous egg lies in the box as still as a stone. It doesn't wobble, no matter how much I stare at it. A chick ready to hatch will tumble around within the shell.

Tolic links his magnifying glass into a loop on his vest. "It'll be a Christmas present, then." He looks askance at my mother, who is ladling hot rice into our breakfast bowls. The eggs I gathered are on the boil. The guava juice glasses are on the table. Mama's mouth is a tight, thin line.

"Thanks, but I've already eaten. I'll wait for you." My friend rushes outside before Papa can start to practice his German.

After breakfast, I grab a rolled-up banana leaf I'd hidden in the jungle. We run to the fishing spot.

Stefan and Ivan are waiting on the riverbank. They stand under our fishing tree, a tamarind with one long branch stretched out over the water.

Blond Stefan is smiling and holding out the waxed rope for us to admire. Husky Ivan is holding out a ball of string and scowling. A long stick with a hook on the end is at their feet.

"Pedrito," Ivan shouts. "Why did you bring the *Germaniya*?"

The Russian word for 'German' sounds like a growl, coming at the end of a sentence in lilting Spanish.

"Leave him alone, Ivan. I invited him."

"*Hola, amigos.*" Stefan ties the end of the rope into a lasso. "May we have good luck today? Did you two bring some bait?" I unroll the banana leaf. Inside are lizard legs. "These have been in the sun since Friday afternoon."

"What did you bring, *Germaniya*?"

"That's enough, Ivan."

Ivan grabs me by the shirt collar. "I'll decide when it's enough."

We're the same height, but Ivan outweighs me by about 30 pounds. I hold the lizard legs under his nose. "Is this enough?"

"Bah! What a stink!"

Ivan stumbles toward the riverbank as Tolic and Stefan admire the fat legs, the putrid stench. The lizard legs are covered in tiny red ants. I put both on the ground and wipe my hands in the dirt to get rid of the ants crawling on my fingers and palms.

Tolic opens the fishing creel. Inside are two chunks of mottled grey, almost translucent fish. "It's from a marlin," he says shyly. "Papa caught it, off the coast of Aruba. Alligators won't care that it's been frozen."

Stefan whistles. "Fish or lizard? Which goes first?"

"You go first, Pedrito." Tolic is eyeing Ivan, who is climbing up the riverbank and glaring.

I use Ivan's string to tie a lizard leg about ten inches above the lasso. Tolic helps me throw it over the low-hanging branch of the tamarind tree. The two of us stand on the riverbank and hold the baited rope with both hands.

The waiting is always hard. Sweat runs down my face and drips off my chin. I forgot to check the horses' blankets and now my bladder is full. Tolic is sweating too, but we don't dare let go of the rope.

As usual, Ivan tries to take charge. "You're not dangling it low enough, Pedrito. It should almost touch the water."

"We're fine," I argue back. "An alligator as far away as Miami could smell that stink."

"Hush," Stefan whispers. "Here they come."

The smooth river water becomes choppy, restless. Flamingoes and other water birds panic and fly to the trees.

Stefan rubs his hands together. "Gater taters."

"You told us to hush," Ivan growls. "You hush."

Stefan laughs. "How's that left foot of yours?"

Ivan scowls.

About a year ago, Ivan had been swimming in the Orinoco River when he tore out of the water, his face rigid in terror. He ran onto the riverbank, screaming in Russian at his left foot. The little toe and the one next to it were gone. Something in the river had bitten them clean off. Bright-red blood spilled onto the riverbank.

Almost immediately, burrowing insects tunneled out of their holes to eat Ivan's blood. Ivan stared at the insects feasting on his foot blood and fainted on the spot. Stefan and I propped his arms across our shoulders and brought him home to his mother. Ivan's wound was clotted with jungle soil. As his mother scrubbed it clean, he woke up whimpering like a baby. He's hated the alligators as bitter enemies ever since.

Ivan has always been a bully, but after the alligator bit his toes off, who could take him seriously? But none of us have gone swimming in the Orinoco River since, no matter how hot it is.

Tolic and I dangle the lizard leg closer to the water. None of us breathes….

The water agitates, with a tell-tale swell on the surface. That's a gator's tail weaving back and forth, ready to propel it straight up into the air.

We all scream, for in a loud burst, a blackish-green alligator thrusts out of the river and lunges for the lizard leg. It's all mouth and teeth. Too late! Tolic and I don't lift the fishing rope fast enough.

In a great splash, the alligator swims away. It has bitten clean through the lasso. The lizard leg is gone.

Now the muddy water is more restless. It bubbles and pops. That means more alligators are swimming toward us.

Ivan pushes us away. "Stand aside. You Poles and Germans know nothing about alligator fishing."

The Russian and Belarusian boys take their turn. Stefan ties another lasso. Ivan wraps the larger chunk of Tolic's marlin ten inches above the lasso and ties it down with the string. They dangle the irresistible treat just above the river. Their timing is perfect—in another great splash, an alligator lunges toward the marlin chunk just as Stefan and Ivan lift the rope. The open-mouthed alligator uses its swishing tail to thrust itself even farther out of the water. Like a launched rocket, it is entirely in the air as it threads through the lasso.

Here comes the luck part—in an airborne panic, a gator will spread its arms and legs as though to swim away from danger.

The alligator, its arms outstretched, begins to lose altitude. The lasso clamps under his front legs. Hand over land, Stefan and Ivan pull rope and beast higher and higher.

The gator twists. It hisses in rage as its tail lashes the air.

"Grab on," Stefan screams. "Help!"

Tolic and I grasp the rope too, as Ivan hooks the alligator and pulls it toward us. We loosen the rope and swing the lassoed gator onto the riverbank. It blinks in surprise; his reptilian brain boggled: how did I end up here?

Stefan brought his baseball bat with him—a second-hand Slugger from Louisville, Kentucky. He grasps the Slugger and lifts it over his head. Ivan pushes Stephan aside, grabs his Slugger, and finishes the job.

"That's how to fish for alligator," Ivan says.

"Good work," Tolic yells back. He hands Ivan his father's long boning knife. Ivan flashes the knife in triumph over his head. He roars as he stomps his feet in a victory dance around the alligator.

We all howl as heroes, as triumphant hunters. DPs look out of their doors and windows. All our little brothers—our *hermanitos*—come running.

It's the tail we want. Stefan divides it into quarters. Alligator meat is white and translucent around the edges. It looks like the ice chip Mama put against my face, so long ago at the mayor's house.

Stefan wraps each share in a banana leaf. Tolic takes his share graciously, but I know the Zimmers won't eat it.

Only then do we take a good look at the alligator. It must have been eight feet long. Its spread front claws are like human hands. Dragon-like spikes push out of its dark back. Its neck and belly are the palest green. The marlin chunk is shredded flesh between two eighteen-inch long rows of teeth.

If we were Yanomani tribesmen, we'd apologize to the alligator for killing it and leaving his children as orphans. "Thank you," I say instead.

The second lizard leg lies on the riverbank, crawling with ants. In minutes nothing will be left but bone. I take the second chunk of marlin out of Tolic's fishing creel and toss it into the river. The water boils up, alligator snouts breach, teeth flash. The marlin chunk disappears down an impossibly-white gator gullet.

“Thank you,” we shout together.

“*Germaniya,* no one can call me a thief.” Ivan throws Tolic’s father’s boning knife at his feet and laughs as he flinches. Stefan and Ivan walk toward the village, their heads held high. *Los hermanitos* follow them.

“Let’s go back to my house,” I say. “We’ll look at my egg again. Maybe it’s wobbling now.”

“Not today.” Tolic holds his share of the alligator tail out to me. “Pedrito, we’re going to Rio de Janeiro in the morning. This meat won’t be good when we return. You can have it.”

“*Muchos gracias, amigo.*” Two chunks of gator tail are enough to feed the five of us for tonight and tomorrow.

Tolic touches my arm. “Perhaps I’ll see your chicken when we return.”

“Perhaps,” I say. “*Feliz Navidad.*” Merry Christmas. I throw my right arm around his shoulder.

“*Feliz Navidad,*” Tolic replies, “*y feliz año nuevo.*” Happy New Year.

With my left arm, I hold my alligator chunks over my head. “Here’s to 1957, it was a good year.”

Mothers with knives are on the riverbank. They’ll cut as much meat as they can from the alligator. The ants will get the rest.

I return home and give Mama both portions of the alligator tail. "It's half the tail," I say, but I don't tell her Tolic gave it to me.

"Could we have gater taters tonight?" I ask.

Mama smiles with tears in her eyes. "Gater taters. Thank you."

It was the *Norte Americano* oil workers who taught the Venezuelans to eat alligator this way. Mama will wash and oil five potatoes and cover them with white-hot charcoal. When the potatoes are ready, Mama will cut the alligator tail into bite-size pieces. She'll season them with salt and cayenne and fry them in hot oil.

We eat the spicy chunks over the hot split potatoes. We have a Sunday Food Feast of gater taters.

After our glorious dinner, Myron pulls on my sleeve. "Come and look at your egg," he says. "It's wriggling."

Papa says, "You'll have something out of that egg for Christmas."

Chapter Seven

Dog

On Christmas Eve afternoon it hatches. It's scrawny, with long yellow legs, an orange beak, scaly-looking skin, and a bony neck. Its dark eyes blink slowly, as though it can't believe this is the world.

It looks like a baby dinosaur but can't be.

"You boys stand back," Papa says. "Let it imprint on Pedrito."

"What does that mean?" Myron asks.

"A baby bird will follow the first living thing it sees. It will think Pedrito is his mother."

Do I want it to follow me?

I crouch down and look at it eye to eye. It blinks. Its huge eyes focus on my face. "*Feliz Navidad,*" I say softly. "Welcome to the family."

It opens its beak. Bwarf.

We all leap back, for this is not the cute, piping sound of a baby chick. It's deep and loud. This sound will not charm Mama.

"*El Perro*!" My three-year-old brother Zenon is jumping up and down. "What's the word in English?"

"'Dog', says Papa.

"He's barking! Dog! Dog!"

Bwarf. Bwarf. It's walking toward me.

Bwarf.

Papa pats me on my back. "Congratulations, Pedrito! You are a mama."

"He's hungry," Zenon says.

Papa, Myron, and Zenon all look at me expectantly. So does the chick.

Bwarf.

Papa gives Myron a coffee cup. "Fetch some cracked corn out of the corn bin in the chicken coop. Let's see if it will eat that."

Myron returns and places the cup in front of Dog. That's what Zenon is already calling it. It's one-quarter full of cracked corn.

Dog eats it all. Bwarf.

"Now Dog wants water," Zenon says.

I place a filled bowl in front of Dog. He scoops water, lifts his neck, and opens his mouth. We watch, fascinated, as the water rolls down his bony throat in a wave. He drinks four times.

"After he eats, you'll have to take him outside to check the horses'
blankets," Papa says.

"But it's raining," I say.

"Use my umbrella."

Mama is standing over Dog. "That's the ugliest thing I've ever seen," she says. "And I survived Hitler's slave camps. Pedrito, if you want it to drink water, you'll have to fetch it yourself. I carry just enough water from the village spigot that we need each day."

Just as Papa said, Dog follows me as I walk out the front door. I hold the umbrella over us and wait. And wait.

Finally, a jet of chalky white lands on the ground under Dog's feet. It is washed away immediately by the pouring rain.

Myron, Zenon, and I marvel at Dog's bedtime routine. Every night, he sleeps in the Pepsi-Cola box next to our bed, and it's always the same.

First, he scratches at the old newspapers Papa has given me for Dog's bed. The shredded paper makes a soft mattress.

Second, he eats a few shreds of the paper as a bedtime snack.

Dog folds his legs under him. He spreads his wings over his body like a blanket. He closes his eyes and yawns mightily. We peer closely at his tongue—a black, two-pronged fork sticking out of his orange beak.

Next, he tucks his head under his right wing. In less than one minute he's fast asleep. His wing feathers flutter as he snores softly.

At dawn he wakes us up with a loud bwarf.

After breakfast, I measure Dog's neck and legs with a ruler. Impossible but true—he's bigger than he was when he went to sleep the night before. By the end of December, his legs were four inches long. On New Year's Day, four and a half inches long.

Today is January 7th, and our school's new term will start after lunch this afternoon. Dog's legs are five inches long.

His neck has grown two inches since he hatched. His wings are longer and broader each morning.

We see the beginnings of real feathers sprouting on his neck, on the tips of his wings, and on his breast.

There's one more important fact about Dog. He likes to be stroked just under his beak and likes it best when I use my index finger. He closes his eyes and sighs. In a few minutes he's fast asleep.

"Maybe you're feeding Dog a special corn," Papa says at breakfast. "I have never seen a rooster grow this fast."

"Super corn," Myron says around a mouthful of rice. "A super corn Superman would eat."

Tolic's papa buys him Superman comic books whenever he's in Caracas. Tolic gives them to me when he's finished reading them. I read them aloud to my brothers. At first, Mama didn't approve but I told her we're learning English when we look at the comics and match the words with the pictures.

Bang! Pow! Punch! A man of steel. We're learning English just fine.

Zenon holds a handful of eggy rice out to Dog.

Bwarf.

Dog gobbles it down before Mama has a chance to scold.

El maize supremo. Super corn. *El arroz supremo.* Super rice.

I worry about Dog. During the worst heat of the day, when the doors and windows are open, he wanders anywhere he pleases, including the jungle.

Dog eats his weight in chicken feed every four days. Mama won't let him eat from our table and Zenon isn't helping by hand feeding him.

"The Buczkowskis do not keep pets," she reminds us at every meal. "Animals are food."

Dog must go into the jungle to hunt for more food. He's always hungry. What if he doesn't come back someday?

This is a new feeling, this worry. It feels like Señor Nicholas's oxen yoke hanging heavy around my neck and no matter how hard I try, I can't shake it off. I catch myself gazing at Mama and Papa in a new light. Surely they don't worry about us in this same way?

Just as Papa predicted, Dog follows my every footstep. Every morning, Dog follows me into the chicken coop when I collect eggs. He waits outside the shower stall for me—dry dust baths on the jungle paths are more to his liking. He struts right into the toilet stall after me and tilts his head curiously.

At breakfast, Dog sits between Zenon and me, because Zenon feeds him eggy rice from his open palm.

"Don't give Dog eggs," Myron exclaims. "He's eating his own brothers and sisters."

Zenon turns to Papa in alarm. "Is that true?"

Papa chews thoughtfully for a moment. "No, I don't think so. These eggs are from other hens. But don't give him your food, Zenon, your mother worries about the three of you getting enough to eat."

"Your father is right," Mama says. "I want all of you to grow up to be…to be…strong young men." Her voice chokes as she turns away. She pulls a dishrag from her pocket and sobs into it.

Papa purses his lips. He lifts his eyebrows at Myron and me.

This is one of Mama's bad days. She's been thinking lately about her own brothers, the three who never had a chance to grow up to be strong young men. She tells us, over and over, that her sons are now the same ages as her brothers were when she lost them forever in the slave camps.

"Finish your breakfast, boys," Papa says softly. "Myron, you're old enough to chop jungle now. You may use Mama's vegetable knife but stay close to me."

"Katrina," he says softer still. "Please don't frighten them. There are no potato slaves in New Barcelona."

"Our boys need to know."

"They know." Papa lifts his hands, palms up. "Katrina, the war has been

over for more than twelve years. We won. I promise you, those *Niemskie swinie* no longer call the tune. Why do you keep bringing up the past?"

I'm not so sure. Those German pigs still wallow in the mud, still smirk at the Buczkowskis.

We finish our breakfasts and brush our teeth.

Papa, Myron, and I go to the jungle's edge, our machetes and Mama's vegetable knife at the ready. Myron is a *Manito* now, a young man. He struts as proudly as a jungle rooster, slicing the air with the knife until Papa tells him to stop, it's not safe.

Every morning the men in our village meet at the jungle's edge, and then hack down the leaves that have crept around the village overnight. Myron holds his head high as he chops. Dog is at my feet, bwarfing and clawing at bugs.

"Every job needs a supervisor," Señor Nicholas mutters while the men laugh. He chops skillfully at banana leaves and palm fronds; they fall into shreds at our feet. "Señor Gallo, is my chopping good enough for you? Tell me, what is your expert opinion?"

The men stop to look at Señor Gallo—at Dog. Each is panting and sweating. They pass around canteens of water.

Dog doesn't answer. Instead, he claws a brown cockroach into three pieces. The parts disappear, still wiggling, down his gullet as the men cheer. Dog claws apart and dines on another, and another.

Is this why Dog is growing so fast? *El cucarachas supremo.*

"Eating cockroaches is a good thing, Pedrito," Señor Napoli says. "Dog can guard your house, and fatten himself up for a magnificent feast. By Easter, he'll be a tasty spring chicken." The rest of the men smack their lips.

Señor Rusanowsky rubs his hands together. "What my Eva could do with your bird! Roasted with onions and potatoes, pickled red cabbage simmering in the rich broth for the soup...."

I gather Dog into my arms. "He's not for eating. He's a pet."

The men shake their heads sadly and chop at the jungle again.

Sometimes I think they're teasing me, these men. Sometimes I think they mean it. What if somebody steals Dog? What if somebody eats him? In New Barcelona, except for Señor Nicholas's oxen, animals are food. Even the best hen can't guard her chick every moment of every day.

Chapter Eight

Hermanito

In the late morning, the boys play in the soccer field in the village common. Dog runs back and forth on the sidelines, bwarfing at us as he referees our games. If a teammate kicks a goal we all raise our arms and cheer. At the same time, Dog raises his wings and flaps toward the soccer ball. We have to grab it quickly, or Dog will try to dribble it down the field and chip it into the jungle.

At lunchtime, my brothers and I dig into our meal of guava juice left over from breakfast, rice, and *cachapas,* Mama's fresh corn pancakes.

Zenon pretends to yawn. He stretches out his arms then lets them drop to his sides. Of course, Dog is there to peck at half a *cachapa* Zenon has dropped on the floor by his feet.

Mama slams her palm on the table. "Zenon! Never do that again! You don't know what it means to starve, to be surrounded by people who have starved to death. Children—your own uncles—STARVED TO DEATH."

Quickly, Zenon scoops a corn pancake off the platter. "Mama, look! A rocket!" he shouts as he rolls it into a tube. Next comes an engine noise—*grrruuummm.* Zenon stuffs the entire *cachapa* in his mouth. His cheeks puff out. As he chews, he looks like a mouse in the corn bin.

Papa says, "Katrina, please. Can't you see you're scaring him?"

Myron and I help Papa harvest his onions and peppers. We brought Zenon to the fields once. Just once—he spent the whole time toddling between the vegetable rows looking for snakes.

Zenon would make a terrible potato slave; any three-year-old would.

I gasp. Those Nazi pigs would never have put up with thousands of three-year-olds, all hungry and crying for their mothers. They killed them. They killed them all.

I had an uncle I'll never meet who was just Zenon's age when those Nazi pigs killed him.

I am so angry I want to smash something, but Mama has five plates, five glasses, five rice bowls, and two cups. There're no extras. Instead, I jump up from my chair and stomp to the front door.

I hear Papa say, "Myron and Pedrito—don't be late for school on the first day of the term."

"Lucky Zenon," Myron mutters around a mighty mouthful. "No school."

I turn and stare at Zenon in surprise. Why didn't I think of this before?

"Zenon, come with me." I take a deep breath as I beckon him toward the chicken coop. Happily, Zenon waddles toward me.

"Would you like to be Dog's mama while I'm in school?"

Zenon frowns. I know *mi hermanito*—my little brother-- so well. Frowning means he's thinking hard. He says, "Dog could be *mi hermanito,* just as I am your *hermanito.*"

I shrug. "Sure, but the important thing is that he has to stay home in the afternoons. You'll have to keep him distracted. That will be your job."

"What does 'distracted' mean?"

"Um…run around in circles. Dog will think it's a game and he'll chase you. Then I can duck out the front door for school."

Dog is at my feet. Zenon gives him a quick pat on the head. "I'm a rocket," he shouts as he raises his arms. Zenon makes engine noises again—"*grrrrum ...grummmmm*"—as he spins in a tight circle.

Dog tilts his head quizzically; his red wattles fling from side to side.

Bwarf. He gives chase and around and around he goes.

I walk to school with anger still churning as hot as chili peppers in my stomach. They're still calling the tune.

In Venezuela, school is open in the afternoons for ten months a year.
Families need their children to work on the farms in the cool, early mornings.

School is school. What's there to say? In our one-room schoolhouse, the smaller children sit in the front row. At our own levels, we study arithmetic, reading, geography, South American history, spelling, and science. Our teacher is Señor Gutiérrez, a young man from Spain.

We older students are finishing our essays about the 19th president of the United States, President Rutherford B. Hayes. Every school in South America has his portrait hanging just above the blackboard.

South American nations have essay contests for their students about President Hayes. Every year, the winners get a cash prize and trips to Washington D.C., and President Hayes's boyhood home, in Delaware, Ohio.

Our teacher wrote President Hayes facts on our chalkboard:

Rutherford Birchard Hayes

From 1864-1870, Uruguay and Paraguay fought over a vast tract of land called the Chaco. Two-thirds of the Paraguayans died in the war, the bloodiest in South American history. Neither side would surrender.

The two nation's leaders sailed to Washington and asked the American president for his judgment.

President Hayes was-given the task of deciding the international boundary between Uruguay and Paraguay. President Hayes gave the Chaco to Paraguay, since they had suffered more in the war.

In your own words, please.

Except for the Uruguayans, South Americans have admired his diplomacy and compassion ever since.

Señor Gutiérrez especially admires the 19th president. "Remember, President Hays ruled in favor of the Paraguayans with complete objectivity. What does 'objectivity' mean?"

Our teacher points to Ivan, who gives him a bored shrug.

"Objectivity? What does it mean?" Señor Nichols's daughter, Maria, raises her hand.

"Señor, it means neutrality."

"Very good, Maria. It didn't matter one way or another to the Americans who won this war.

"Remember, too, the Americans had just fought a terrible civil war, fought at just about the same time as the Uruguayan and Paraguayan war. President Hayes had been a brigadier-general in that war and had been wounded four times. He knew suffering first hand, and wanted the suffering to end. What else did he do?"

My brother shoots his hand in the air.

"Yes, Myron Buczkowski?"

"Señor, he gave the Paraguay River to the Paraguayans. The Bolivians and Paraguayans are the only people in South America who do not have an ocean coastline. The Paraguay River gives the Paraguayans a water route to the Atlantic Ocean."

"Very good. Both sides were satisfied. Anything else?" Our teacher's eyebrows shoot up in surprise. "Ivan Kirsanowsky?"

We turn our heads toward the back row. Ivan never raises his hand.

Ivan sneers. "Lucy Hayes did not allow card playing, alcohol, dancing, or smoking in her husband's White House. She was known as 'Lemonade Lucy.' "

"That's right." Our teacher's voice falters a bit. He claps his hands. "You may take a thirty-minute recess."

At recess, Sophie Orcziechowski and Elizabeth Rusanowosky like to sit together under a shade tree. Their heads are together as they leaf through tattered movie magazines: *Photoplay, Modern Screen,* and *Silver Screen.*

Elizabeth's father is New Barcelona's barber. He has subscriptions, and he allows Elizabeth to bring the tattered back copies to school. Everyone in town has seen these magazines, even Papa, who claims to read only newspapers.

Elizabeth Taylor. Kim Novak. Marilyn Monroe. Natalie Wood and Robert Wagner. James Dean. Marlon Brando. Montgomery Cliff. The actor-singers Frank Sinatra, Dean Martin, Sammy Davis, and Elvis Presley. Everyone knows these faces as well as they know the faces of their own families. The American movie stars in the photos flash brilliant white teeth, clear eyes, perfect complexions, and shining, perfectly curled hair.

Sophie points to Elizabeth Taylor. "I want her violet eyes."

Elizabeth points to Marilyn Monroe. "I want her blond hair."

They both point to Robert Wagner and say, "I want Natalie Wood's husband." They giggle as I roll my eyes toward Ivan and Stefan.

"Girls," Ivan says in disgust.

Señor Gutiérrez calls us back inside. We settle into our seats and wait for him to begin the next class. Instead, our teacher points to the portrait of President Rutherford B. Hayes above the blackboard.

"I want you all to understand something. Yes, there is much to admire about the United States of America. There is much to admire about Venezuela as well. What other nation in South America has taken in so many European refugees from the Second World War? Venezuela leads the continent. What other nation in South America has hired so many teachers from Spain, like myself, to come into the jungle and teach the children of these refugees? Again, Venezuela leads the continent.

"What other nation has given so many college scholarships to the children of these Displaced Persons? Again, Venezuela--"

"*Hermanito,*" Zenon calls from the schoolyard.

"Oh no," I whisper. "Not Dog."

"I know what the Venezuelans call you," our teacher says, a bit louder. "Delayed Pilgrims," he says in English before switching back to Spanish. "But the

Venezuelan government wants all of you to stay. Build a better Venezuela for the 21st century. Your country needs you."

"*Hermanito,* come back. Come back, *hermanito.*"

Go home, Zenon, I think. Take Dog with you.

Our teacher looks out the window. "Who is this toddler's younger brother? Who is his *hermanito*?"

I groan.

For a fraction of a second, Zenon's smiling face pops into the open window. "Pedrito," he says before his feet hit the ground again. His voice floats through the schoolhouse window. "Mama made me take a nap after lunch. Dog got away while I was asleep. *Mi hermanito* wants his mama."

Bwarf.

Dog jumps onto the open window ledge. Bwarf. Bwarf. He gives everyone a fierce stare. Girls scream. Boys yell. Señor Gutiérrez holds his pointer as a drawn sword in front of him for protection.

Dog flaps across the school room. He lands on my President Rutherford B. Hayes essay.

"Go home, Dog."

Bwarf.

Dog yawns mightily. "No," I shout. "It's not bedtime."

I watch in horror as Dog's claws tear at the lined pages. He shreds them and gobbles some of the tatters as though they are *el maize supremo*.

"Not my essay," I cry out. "Bad Dog! Bad Dog!"

He stretches his neck and spreads his wings.

Zenon dashes into school and pulls my rooster off my desk. "I'm sorry, Pedrito. See you at dinner." Zenon takes off toward the door. Dog is looking back at me, sleepy-eyed, from over Zenon's shoulder.

Señor Gutiérrez lifts up the shreds of what's left of my essay. They drift through his fingers and settle on the dirt floor.

Señor Gutiérrez asks, "Your rooster's name is Dog?"

"I'm sorry, Señor. His cackle sounds like a dog's bark and…"

"I see. Pedrito, what has just happened here? Can you tell me?"

"Señor, I'm sorry. Dog hatched on Christmas Eve…"

"No, no, no, Pedrito. You can't guess?" My teacher grins at me. "Then I will tell you. For the first time in all my years of teaching, a student can say this truthfully: The dog ate my homework."

Chapter Nine

La Serpiente de Cascabel

At sunrise in late March…

As always, my mother wakes me. "Pedrito, go to the chicken coop. Why are they so noisy today?"

The chickens are squawking loudly. Even Papa is awake on the one morning a week he gets to sleep until after dawn. He's sitting up in bed and rubbing his eyes. My father groans as he tries to straighten his back. The vertebras creak and crack one by one. Papa is still a young man, but he has the hunched-over back of a farmer of sixty.

"Take your machete with you, Pedrito," he reminds me. "The chickens are squawking to high heaven."

Zenon pops up in bed. “Maybe it’s another Dog!”

“Just what we need,” Mama grumbles, “another Dog.”

Since Dog ate my homework, we’ve had to shut the doors and windows on weekday afternoons. Papa, Mama, Zenon, and Dog sit in the stifling heat and darkness, but at least Dog can’t disrupt school.

Dog accompanies me to the chicken coop every morning. All I have to do is open the door, and the hens cluck a soft welcome to him. As he struts down the aisle, the *gallinas* are soothed by his presence.

But not today—they squawk louder, as if asking Dog for help.

As always, I hold up my candle to check the whitewashed walls for bird spiders, scorpions, and lizards. Nothing. The floorboards? Nothing but Dog’s black claws shining in the candlelight.

“Bird brains,” I mutter. “There’s nothing wrong.”

Suddenly, Dog stops in mid-stride. He doesn’t bark. Instead, he turns his face toward the far wall. He puffs up his feathers to make him look twice his size. What comes from his throat sounds like a low growl.

The chickens stop fussing. All I hear is Dog’s menacing growl--*bwarrrr.*

My hands are shaking as I point the candlelight toward the far wall. There it is—the unique diamond scales of snakeskin. A huge snake coils up twice, thrice, four times. As it raises its head, the eyes glow red in the candlelight.

What I hear next makes my blood run cold. It is the unmistakable sound—like the jittery noise of maracas shaken much too fast—of a rattlesnake's tail.

La serpiente de cascabel—the serpent of the little bell—rattles a deadly warning to Dog, to me, and to the silent, still hens. The cold, red eyes turn toward me….

Bwarf.

In an instant, Dog flaps high above the snake's head. It strikes at Dog, but my rooster is just out of reach. Dog flaps against the far wall. The snake's head curves away from me and strikes at Dog once more. Once more it misses, but this time my machete slices down to the floorboards, just behind the snake's head. The snake's head separates from its body in a gush of blood. Yet the body still coils and side winds toward me.

I turn and flee. My knees kick the door open. As I jump out of the coop, a thunderclap of panicked *gallinas* escapes with me. They squawk and beat their wings around my head.

Papa bumps into me. "What on earth?"

"A rattlesnake! Dog saved me. He pretended to attack it."

"Put your arms down. You'll cut me or one of the chickens to shreds swinging that machete. Or you'll burn yourself with the candle."

I drop my arms. One by one, the chickens flap to the ground. As though nothing had happened, they peck at the dirt, looking for insects. Dog is still in the coop, growling.

Papa takes the candle from my hand. He looks inside the coop, and then with a yelp springs out of it.

Our gazes meet and concur.

"I'll collect the eggs, today. Don't tell your mother."

"Don't tell your mother what?" Mama calls from the back door. "A snake?"

"Not a big one," Papa replies. "Everything's fine."

"Mama," I say, "Dog saved me. I've never seen such bravery."

Zenon is standing next to Mama. "Papa, may I see the snake?"

"No," Papa and I say together.

I wash the snake's blood off my hands in our shower stall. Something catches my gaze. I stare at my feet. For a fleeting moment I think—chocolate? For in the pearly half-light of dawn, my feet look like they're covered in flecks of melted chocolate. Not chocolate, blood. Snake blood.

"Just a minute," I call to my family. I kick off my shoes as I turn the shower on full blast. I can't wash the blood off fast enough.

How quickly does the news of a decapitated rattlesnake in a New Barcelona chicken coop travel? Faster than lightning.

We haven't even finished our breakfasts before Stefan and Ivan are at the back door. Myron is staring at me, wide-eyed. Zenon is feeding Dog eggy rice while chattering away about snakes.

Mama is not scolding Zenon about feeding Dog. Instead, she's all smiles. "Stefan and Ivan," she purrs as she opens the back door. "Come in, come in. Have some breakfast."

My family looks at her in shock. Mama doesn't share food.

"We have already eaten, Señoría Buczkowski," Ivan replies. He stares at the juice pitcher.

"Have some guava juice. I insist. I squeeze it fresh every morning."

"*Muchas gracias*, Señora Buczkowski," Stefan replies.

Mama scrubs her glass and Papa's. She pours guava juice into the two clean glasses. She likes to save the rest of the guava juice for our lunch each noon, but I say nothing.

Good news is just like bad news, I suppose. It takes a while for both to sink in. I killed a rattlesnake with my machete. Dog helped, but I killed it. I think about those red eyes staring at me so coldly and my heart pounds fast.

My friends drink their juice as my mother asks about their families. They reply politely but never take their gaze off me. In a few minutes, we are standing outside the back door. Myron has tagged along.

Stefan pulls a cloth sack from his pocket. "Where is the snakehead?"

"If my father hasn't thrown it into the jungle, it's still in the chicken coop."

Papa has left the coop door open. One by one, those stupid chickens have returned to their nests. At dawn, a hungry rattlesnake could have eaten them. Now they're brooding on their nests again, as if it had never been there.

Idiot bird-brains, I think, but at the same time I remember how clever Dog was. He fooled the snake.

He made the snake turn its back to me. All those mornings of dissecting cockroaches while the men chop at the jungle—did Dog figure out how sharp machetes are? Just like his claws?

Dog is smart enough to make that connection.

I close the coop door so Dog can't follow us. Stefan, Ivan, and Myron follow me to the very back of the coop. "Here it is," I say softly, as though the snakehead were only sleeping.

Stefan whistles.

"That head is bigger than my foot," Ivan says breathlessly. "Your father killed that snake, not you."

"Which foot?" Stefan taunts. "Your left foot's toes are bit off."

Ivan slugs him. "Shut up."

"We have to take this snakehead to Tolic," Stefan says. "He has to see it. Where's the body?"

A streak of blood on the floorboards is all the remains of the snake's body. "I did so kill it, Ivan. Papa must have picked it up, thrown it into the jungle. Dog distracted it and I killed it."

Dappled sunlight shines through the knotholes in the coop walls. Myron, my friends, and I look at one another. I know what I'm thinking—something bigger than the snake has dragged it into the jungle for breakfast. A jaguar, a boar, or perhaps some massive beast none of us has ever heard of. In the mottled light, I see the flicker of fear in their eyes.

"To the Zimmers,' I say.

"May I go too?" Myron pleads. "Pedrito, please?"

I look to Ivan and Stefan. They shrug. They too, have *hermanitos* who trot at their heels like puppies.

By the time we call out to Tolic and cross his bridge, the cloth sack is dripping blood. Dog walks behind Ivan and pecks at it. Myron, and Stefan's and Ivan's four little brothers tag behind us.

Tolic is waiting for us on the front lawn. "What is it?" he asks, eyeing the dripping sack.

Ivan laughs. "Look at this, *Germaniya.* Ivan flips open the sack; the snakehead tumbles out at Tolic's feet.

I pick up Dog so he can't attack the snakehead.

Tolic doesn't flinch, not this time. Instead, he pulls his magnifying glass out of his vest loop. He kneels next to the snakehead for a better look. "A rattler, all right. We have to give this snakehead to the Yanomani."

The rest of us flinch.

Chapter Ten

The Yanomani

The Yanomani tribesmen live in the deep jungles of Brazil and Venezuela. They believe a rattlesnake doesn't know it's dead if its head hasn't been buried by their medicine men. The living-dead rattlesnake will seek everlasting revenge on those who killed it. That means Dog and me.

Tolic stands up and holds his hand out to Ivan.

I groan. "That's just a superstition, Tolic. The snake's dead."

Ivan crosses his arms in front of his chest. The cloth sack drops to his feet. "Russians do not like the Yanomani. The Yanomani do not like Russians. Even such a gift as this," he nudges the snakehead with his boot, "will not sweeten their opinion of us."

Stefan sighs. “You know we have to give them the head, Pedrito.”

“I need the sack, Ivan,” Tolic says.

“The snake’s dead,” I argue. “The medicine men don’t know I killed it. They don’t know Dog had a hand in killing it.”

“What if they find out?” Tolic argues back. “A *Blanco* killed a giant rattler in the *Blanco* village. His jungle rooster—a pet—helped kill it. You don’t think the Yanomani will find out? You don’t think they’ll be angry because we didn’t think it was important enough to give it to them? We don’t believe the snake is still alive, but they do.”

The snakehead is at our feet. Its eyes are milky-white, dull. Tiny red ants are crawling in and out of its mouth.

I point to the head. “Doesn’t it look dead to you guys?”

“Of course, it does,” Stefan replies. “But the snake isn’t dead to the Yanomani. If the snake can’t find you and Dog, it’ll come after them.”

“I-I don’t believe that,” I stammer. I look at the snake head again. Beetles are crawling out of the ground to eat it, just like they did with Ivan’s foot blood.

This is the Yanomani's jungle, after all. What if they're right about a rattlesnake—the serpent of the little bell? Everlasting revenge.

Stefan says, "We need to go to the Yanomani village today."

I shake my head. "I can't go today. Myron, Zenon, and I take my father's vegetables to market on Saturdays."

Myron speaks up, "We'll go tomorrow."

"Tomorrow morning, first thing," Tolic says. "I'll hide this snakehead in the
freezer, behind the leg of lamb Mama ordered for Easter dinner."

Myron asks, "Won't your mother see it?"

Tolic shakes his head. His eyes have a furtive, hidden quality to them. I know my best friend so well—he doesn't want to explain about his family's cook in front of Ivan. Mama's words—rich Nazis—still sting in Tolic's ears.

"Does everyone have a leather umbrella?" Tolic asks. "We have extras."

We all nod as we gaze at the snakehead. The leather umbrella is for shade, but it has a more important role. The bright green arrow snake will nose-dive right out of the jungle canopy to bite a neck, or a shoulder blade, or an upper arm. An arrow snake's bite will kill a grown man in thirty seconds.

The leather umbrella will slow them down, sometimes. Arrow snakes have been known to bounce off the umbrellas and land on the jungle floor. This gives the people on the trail enough time to run before the stunned arrow snake comes to and bites an ankle.

"We'll meet here after breakfast," Tolic says. "Hot chocolate before we leave for the Yanomani village."

Ivan scowls. I know how much he likes hot chocolate.

"You're not going, Myron," I say in my best Papa's voice. "It's too dangerous."

Bug-eyed, Myron just nods. Stefan's and Ivan's little brothers nod, too. *Los hermanitos* will stay home.

After lunch, Myron, Zenon, and I load Papa's vegetables into Señor Nicholas's oxen cart. We sell Papa's crop in the neighboring village's market square. Señor Nicholas buys us shave ice cones. It seems like an ordinary, pleasant Saturday afternoon, Zenon chattering away like a monkey until he falls asleep in the oxen cart on the way home.

But Myron and I are subdued.

New Barcelona adults speak in murmurs about the Yanomani. Our parents say the tribesmen live in a constant state of war—half of their men are killed in combat.

The Yanomani are rumored to be cannibals. The mayor has warned the DPs, again and again, to stay out of their parts of the jungle. In even more hushed voices, our parents speak of this as well.

I turn to Myron, "After breakfast tomorrow, tell Mama and Papa I'm at the Zimmers. Dog can't go with me. The Yanomani will want his feathers. Zenon will have to keep him distracted."

At Food Feast tonight, Mama doesn't scold Zenon as he feeds Dog corn pancake. Come to think of it, she didn't scold Zenon this morning either, as he fed Dog eggy rice. Mama's hands are trembling as she uses her fork and spoon. Instead of scowling at Dog, she looks at him with approval and respect.

I know my family so well, we all live in the same room after all. Papa must have told Mama about the monster, the *serpiente de cascabel* among the *gallenas*, and how Dog risked his life to save mine.

Early Sunday morning, in a half an hour by Tolic's wristwatch, we are in the Yanomani village, at least what used to be their village. The fire rings are cold. Yanomani live in a *shabono*, a common open-air shelter. No food baskets crowd the shade under the *shabono*. The roof itself has tears in it. With relentless speed, the jungle is reclaiming their fields.

Papa once explained it at a Saturday Food Feast. "Rainforest soil is dark, but it only looks fruitful. In fact, jungle soil is as unfertile as sand because of the bacteria, always eating away at the nutrients. The poor soil must be why the Yanomani are in a constant state of war.

"They're always moving house, always encroaching upon another village's territory. How sad," Papa had sighed as he helped himself to more of Mama's good *bischoho*. "All that bloodshed and all they need is a good fertilizer."

"Over here!" Tolic calls to us. "I've found a new trail. This must lead to their new village."

In minutes we see new fields cut out of the jungle. As a farmer's son, I recognize sweet potato, sweet peppers and hot peppers, mango, papaya, corn, sugar cane, and coffee plants.

These Yanomani are just finishing a new *shabono* made of long strips of tree bark. A *shabono* is egg-shaped; they all live under the roof together.

We've been spotted—instantly, shrill cries rise up among the women and girls. The howler monkeys high in the tree canopy echo their shrieks. In seconds, it's too loud to hear what Stefan is saying, even though he's shouting in my ear.

Yanomani men rush up, each holding a spear. Tolic, Stefan, and I smile but we keep a careful eye on their spear points.

The spear points are coated with beeswax. The beeswax is poisoned from the skin of tree frogs. The toxic tree frogs are no bigger than a peso. They live in thimble-size pools of water within the broad leaves of the jungle. Vivid red, orange, yellow, green, and blue—I've never been close enough to any of them to know which are the most deadly.

Slowly, very slowly, we lower our leather umbrellas and drop them behind us. Tolic holds out the snakehead cupped in his gloved hands. The men jump back as they shout. One runs to the *shabono* and brings back with him their *chaman,* their medicine man. The *chaman* wears a halo of bright green and blue parrot feathers. Around his shoulders is a necklace of fiery red and gold rooster feathers.

One by one, the women and girls stop shrieking. One by one, the howler monkeys stop shrieking.

The men are wearing the red face dye than comes from the *onoto* plant. Each has charcoal rubbed onto his arms and shoulders, like tattoos. They have long, straight black hair, oiled and wrapped around their heads. Their skin is the same reddish-brown as their baskets.

Tolic gives the medicine man the snakehead. He drops it with a shout. The Yanomani men glare at us, their spears at the ready. My heart beats faster than when I first saw the rattler's cold red eyes.

"It's still frozen," Tolic says. "They don't know what frozen is."

"I'll pick it up," I say softly. "I'll pantomime a machete." I lift my eyebrows. Very slowly, I raise my right index finger to mean, Please wait one minute, Señores. "*Un momento, por favor*." Instead, the men tip their chins up to look at the sky. They frown quizzically.

"Pedrito, they don't know what a minute is," Stefan says.

My mind races—an index finger as a substitute for the minute hand, the clock face itself, measured time, a polite request for more time, a freezer with an icy snakehead hidden out of sight behind a frozen leg of lamb for Tolic's Easter dinner, the sons of Eastern European DPs from the Second World War—I can only guess at the vast gulf between them and us.

Slowly, I lift the snakehead with my left hand. I pretend to hold a machete with my right, and pretend to cut the snake's head off with it. The freezing snakehead feels like it's burning into my palm. Its middle is still frozen solid. Just under the skin, the flesh feels crunchy, for the ice crystals have not yet thawed.

"Don't flinch," Tolic whispers. "No fear."

I press my elbow to my side and force my left hand steady. I hold the snakehead out to the *chaman.* Gingerly, he takes it and gasps. I nod to him and he nods back, admiration in his eyes. Quickly, he puts the snakehead into a basket at his feet. As the Yanomani men talk among themselves, each looks at us and nods in a friendly way.

We nod in a friendly way back to them.

The *chaman* holds out something to Tolic. It is a small pouch, like a cozy watchpocket but to be worn around the wrist or ankle. The tanned leather looks as soft as butter.

"*Muchos gracias,*" Tolic says politely. "*Danke.*" Thank you.

"*Vamanos,*" Stefan says. Let's go.

The *chaman* reaches out and touches Stefan's butter-bright hair. Stefan's yellow curls twine around his finger tips. He holds Stefan's forearms into the sunlight. The arm hair glimmers as gold. The men nod and talk to one another excitedly.

"*Buenos dias*," Stefan says softly. I know he's trying with everything he's got not to turn tail and run in terror.

The *chaman* laughs and points to Stephan's light blue eyes.

"*Vamanos, amigos*," I whisper.

Slowly, we reach behind us for our umbrellas. Still smiling, we back into the forest, and force ourselves to walk not run, as the howler monkeys begin to shriek once more in the jungle canopy high above our heads.

Chapter Eleven
A Circle Opens

It's June, and Dog is almost full-grown, almost 30 pounds.

His breast and tail feathers are golden yellow. His wings and back are jungle green. Brilliant red feathers line his throat. His leg feathers are the same shiny brownish-yellow of the plantains that grow around our village. His razor-sharp claws are the same sparkling black as the starry night sky.

Dog guards our home with the fierce instincts of born predator. Every morning he secures the perimeter, paying close attention to the dark corners in the kitchen. Four times a week—sometimes more—we hear his low, menacing growl. The growl means he's found something that isn't supposed to be here. Once he's found his quarry, his hard hunter's stare never looks away from it.

Bwarrrrrrr.

We were eating breakfast last Wednesday. Ever since *la serpiente de cascabel,* we've learned to freeze when Dog utters this half-caw, half-growl. As protection when he hunts, Dog pulls his head back, his wings cover his heart.

He'd strutted slowly toward the kitchen corner near the water bucket.

We were all holding our guava juice glasses to our lips.

"What has he found this time, Pedrito?" Zenon had asked.

"Nobody moves," Mama said. "Let him hunt."

As quick as lightning, Dog's claws struck at something. He ran toward the open doorway with a wriggling spider in his beak.

"Look at the size of that spider!" Myron shouted.

Mama screamed and jumped onto her chair.

Myron, Zenon, and I ran through the open front door as Dog sprinted into the jungle with his prize. "There he goes. There he goes," I said. Only his bobbing tail feathers were visible on the jungle trail, glinting golden between the leaves and bright flowers.

He hides in the jungle to eat whatever he's caught, as the birds in the canopy clamor above him, demanding their share.

"Boys," Papa called out the front door. "Come back here and finish your breakfasts."

We sat down to our eggs and rice, still warm.

As I ate, I studied Mama.

On the one hand, she's horrified of what Dog finds in the corners. It's always something toxic—a scorpion, a spider the size of Papa's hand, or an eight-inch long centipede. On the other hand, she's glad Dog catches them.

Before Dog, these creatures had the run of the house. They scurried from dark corner to dark corner as we sat at our table to eat, as we did our homework, as Papa read his newspapers. They climbed up the bedposts as we slumbered, and Mama was as innocent as an infant in her ignorance.

There was nothing in Mama's Polish childhood—nothing—like these outsized and poisonous insects. One kerosene lamp isn't bright enough to light our entire hut. Sometimes I catch her wringing her hands and glancing from side to side. What else lurks in the dark corners, poised to strike?

Just yesterday morning, Dog caught a rat near the potato bin. He grabbed it by the neck and shook it hard to kill it. As Mama screamed, Dog raced out the front door with his prize, Myron, Zenon, and I running to catch up.

Once again, Dog's golden tail feathers bobbed as he ran down the jungle trail. From the canopy the jungle birds wheedled Dog, demanding that he share his breakfast with them.

"When are we going to follow him, Pedrito?" Myron asked. "When are we going to see where Dog goes?"

"Leave him alone," I said. "He's our protector."

And on this morning...

Dog is strutting silently between the furniture and the walls, as usual. If he doesn't find something—a cockroach, a termite, or even a beetle, his eyes snap in anger. His eyes are snapping this morning.

Mama steps from the stove with her rice bowl in her hands. She places it on the floor between Zenon and me. Dog has learned that good things to eat land between Zenon and myself. He runs right over.

"I know Dog likes corn," she says. "Perhaps he'd like a cornmeal mush for breakfast."

Dog pecks at the cooled mush. He eats every drop.

Mama, sharing food? Mama, feeding an animal with her own rice bowl?

Bwarf.

“That’s Dog’s way of thanking you, Mama,” Zenon says.

“He’s very welcome. Dog’s a good hunter,” she replies. “This house is much safer when he’s on the prowl.”

“To our survival.” Papa lifts his juice glass.

“To our liberation.” Mama lifts her juice glass.

I lift my juice glass. To Dog, I think, for he has finally won Mama over.

“This Saturday, I’m going to buy Dog his own bowl,” Mama says, “at the Puerto de Cruz market place. Isn’t that a good idea, Karol?”

Papa can only nod. He’s as flabbergasted as me.

“Doesn’t Dog look funny?” Mama asks me with a smile. “When he runs out the door with his quarry, I’d swear he’s thinking he doesn’t want to share his breakfast with the Buczkowskis. He needs a tin bowl.”

“He does look funny, Mama.” I smile back.

“Those feathers are called iridescent, as though they’re shimmering with electricity,” Mama says.

"Ir-i-des-cent," Zenon repeats carefully. "Ir-i-des-cent."

After Dog killed the rattlesnake, Mama changed, bit by bit, and for the better. She accepted Dog as a member of our family. She opened our circle and welcomed a stranger in. What tumbled out of that circle was some of her anger, her bitterness, and some of her fear.

What was it like, this sea change for the better? To me, it was all about the weather and the sky.

In the months of August and September, hurricanes and heavy rain sweep in from the Atlantic Ocean and pummel our village. The rain hammers against our tin Quonset hut and makes such a racket we can't hear ourselves speak. For days and nights, the howling wind wallops New Barcelona. It knocks over chicken coops, shower stalls, and outhouses. The swollen Oronoco River roars in our ears day and night.

Rainwater floods our floor with jungle silt, drowned insects, and mud. Just when we think we can't stand another minute, just when we think we're ready to pick up and move someplace, any place, the heavy weather stops. Within a day the sun comes out, the temperature lowers to a comfortable seventy-five degrees, and the air turns dry and clear.

For my family, Mama's change was like end of hurricane season, except we didn't know such an end was possible. None of us knew we'd lived under an onslaught for our entire lives.

That's the weather, here's the sky.

A year ago, Herr Zimmer took Tolic and me to Angel Falls, in southeastern Venezuela. The cook had loaded the trunk of Herr Zimmer's Maybach Zeppelin touring automobile with picnic baskets, canteens filled with ice water, blankets, insect repellant, and medicine. The chauffer had checked and re-checked the tires, the gasoline, the oil, and the shocks.

The twelve-cylinder touring car puttered out of the Zimmer's driveway, and then bellowed onto the dirt road like a great beast.

Startled locals and their braying donkeys leapt out of our way as the chauffer shifted into the higher gears and the throttle roared.

The 1936 Maybach Zeppelin has slender brass flower vases bolted onto the frame, to the right and left of the passenger seats. Frau Zimmer had arranged some of her orchids in the vases, to celebrate our grand adventure. We laughed as the Maybach Zeppelin bounced out of the potholes, for each time, the water in the vases sloshed onto the black leather seats.

"*Macht schnell*," Herr Zimmer shouted. Faster, faster....

The chauffer tuned the radio to a jazzy Caracas station. Tolic and I drank iced Pepsi-Cola and lemonade from a cooler built right into the car. Herr Zimmer drank chilled champagne right out of the bottles. Lunch and dinner were hard-cooked eggs, fresh pineapple, potato salad, jars of picked herring in sour cream, pickles, salmon steaks with dill sauce, fine Argentine beef, rye bread, chocolate cake, and *la Galletas de ángel*--angel cookies.

"Our cook knows you like her angel cookies, Pedrito," Tolic said. "She made them just for you."

The chauffer pitched our tent in the national park. As we nodded off, he swathed mosquito netting around and around the tent like a cocoon. We slept like rocks, and had more hard-cooked eggs, chocolate cake, and Brazilian coffee for breakfast.

After lunch, we hiked for a two hours to the lookout point for Angel Falls.

It wasn't the stunning luxury of the expedition, or the 3,212 foot waterfall—the highest in the world—that made me gape in astonishment.

It was the sky, for high above the jungle canopy, the baby-blue sky over Angel Falls is endless, endless. Entire cloud formations floated toward the setting sun.

The sun—I'd never seen an actual sunset before—glowed reddish-orange before sinking into the west over Columbia and toward the Pacific Ocean. As the sun set, the sky turned cobalt, then indigo, then navy. The stars appeared, thousands upon thousands of them in the wide-open sky.

"The sky, the sky," I kept repeating. "Look at the sky."

"There's an airplane flying south," Herr Zimmer called out in German. He pointed a wobbly champagne bottle to what looked like a formation of moving stars in the black sky. "It must be going to Rio de Janeiro, or Buenos Aries. From where could that plane be flying? Miami? Washington? New York City? Dallas?"

Herr Zimmer was also wobbly on his feet. Tolic helped him to a bench. "Papa, how many bottles is that? Haven't you had enough?"

"The sky, Tolic. Look at the sky."

"*Si, amigo,*" Tolic said slowly, as though speaking to a child. "I see it."

Our guide lit the Coleman kerosene lanterns, made in Wichita, Kansas. We returned to the campsite. The next morning we went home, with plenty of food left over to give to Mama. We had a Food Feast for five nights in a row, with meat every night.

Amigos, we Buczkowskis stepped into the clear, calm weather of Mama's better nature as something amazing, true enough. But our astonished thankfulness was as boundless as that sky.

Chapter Twelve
Stefan

It is high summer, and Stefan has not been in school for days. After breakfast, Ivan and I go to his house.

Stefan's mother speaks in a jumbled panic. I listen closely, but I hear nothing that sounds remotely like Polish. Ivan tries to translate for me but she speaks much too quickly.

Ivan keeps shaking his head. In Russian, he speaks slowly, and says the same words again and again. Stefan's mama doesn't take the hint. In her Belarus dialect, she speaks faster, faster. Soon her words are choking with sobs.

Ivan scratches his head. "I think she's saying that Stefan has had a fever for three days." Ivan likes to play the part of Ilya Muromets, the Russian strongman-giant from the folk tales, the killer of dragons, but I can tell he's worried about his best friend.

"Ask her if she has been getting ice from the mayor's house."

Ivan asks her about the ice. Stephan's mother nods.

Ivan and I stare at our friend. In summer, the hottest time of the year, everyone is red-faced and sweaty. Each time I draw breath, wet air flows hot into my lungs, like breathing in steam from a singing tea kettle. The daily soccer game ends early and people stay indoors, away from the terrible heat.

Stefan's face is as dry as ashes, like a piece of chalk from our school's blackboard. Why isn't he sweating to cool down? Heat pours off him.

"*Amigo*," I say, "you'd better get well soon. Señor Gutiérrez is piling on the homework." Stefan just looks at me with vacant eyes.

Stefan's mother wraps ice in washcloths and places them on his forehead and in his armpits. He doesn't even wince.

"What's wrong with him?" Ivan asks. "Do you know, Señoría Bliatok? A sickness? An insect bite? Where has the fever come from?"

His mother just shakes her head and begins to cry again. Ivan and I say *adios* to Stefan and leave together.

Ivan and I stand in the shade of the barber shop. His face must mirror mine. His is wide-eyed, staring at nothing, and slack-jawed in shock. His hands ball into fists.

Stefan's family is from Belarus, a small nation next to Poland. Belarus lost half its population from 1930-1950. First, the Russian Communists invaded and killed the people they didn't like, and then the Nazis did the same, and finally immigration took those strong enough to leave.

I ask myself this all the time: Where was God in Poland? Maybe He was too busy in Belarus? Stefan's family is a miracle. Stefan is a miracle.

Venezuela is different, isn't it? I'm no a potato slave. I live in the New World, in a town run by a friendly mayor who has annual Christmas party for everyone. Here our parents found a fresh start. People aren't supposed to die. Not here in Venezuela.

I never thought I'd lose anybody.

I snap my fingers. "The Yanomani medicine man, their *chaman.* We gave him the rattlesnake head. He was fascinated with Stefan's blond hair. Remember I told you?"

"So?"

"So…what if the *chaman* man knows what's wrong with Stefan? What if he has some jungle medicine that will cure him?"

Ivan grunts. "A Yanomani will know what's wrong with Stefan? Really?"

"We could carry him on a stretcher."

Ivan just shakes his head.

"Their new village is only about forty minutes from here."

Ivan shakes his head again. "The Yanomani don't like Russians, and Russians don't like the Yanomani."

"You won't help your best friend? I'll cross the Zimmer's bridge and get Tolic. We'll all persuade the Bliatoks to bring Stefan to the medicine man."

Ivan shudders. "They make my skin crawl. They're cannibals. When look at me in the marketplace…they see me as something good to eat, I think."

"We're all afraid of the Yanomani, Ivan."

"I can't go, Pedrito. Sorry." Ivan's green eyes shine bright with terror.

I stomp my foot. "Ilya Muromets, the giant who kills dragons. Who rips trees out of the forest with his bare hands? What a joke!"

Ivan ducks his head. "They don't like Russians."

"Bullies are cowards."

Ivan mutters something, a jawful of Russian. I know what he said.

"'We all suffer.' You Russians say that all the time. My mother screams her nightmares every night."

"Your parents. Bah!" Ivan spits on the ground. "Your parents lived on rats and potatoes in a forced labor camp. They lived like kings! My parents lived on sawdust after the Nazis surrounded their city for a thousand days."

"*Si*, the Siege of Stalingrad. Those Nazi pigs."

"*Si,* those Nazi pigs."

"Ivan, those Nazis are the reason we all ended up here, in Venezuela, in the Amazon River basin."

"*Si.*"

"Those Nazi pigs are the reason Stefan is sick. What if he dies? They're still calling the--"

Ivan shoves me against the barbershop window. The back of my head hits the window—hard.

My heart pounds as we stare at each other—one, two, three, four….

How did Ivan get so tall all of a sudden? He's always outweighed me, now he's a good three inches taller, too. Ivan's face is chili pepper red. His mouth is a snarl of yellow teeth. His draws his right fist back....

"I'm going to f-f-f-fetch Tolic. Stick around to translate. Can you do that for your best friend?"

Ivan lets me go. He trots off toward home.

When I return with Tolic, Ivan is standing outside of the Bliatoks' hut. He's staring at the grass.

"Translate what I say to Señor Bliatok. Can you do that?"

He shrugs.

Of course, Stefan's father is outraged. "My father was Dean of Medicine at the University of Minsk! He would be horrified if he knew his grandson was going to a witch doctor for treatment. Jungle medicine—bits of bone rattling in a dried gourd. And some chanting. It's beyond imagining."

Señoría Bliatok is pulling at her husband's sleeve. This gives me hope.

I continue. "If Stefan has caught an Amazonian disease, the Yanomani *chaman* will know what it is. He'll know how to cure it."

After Ivan translates, Señor Bliatok throws his hands above his head. "The University of Minsk, one of the finest medical schools in Europe!"

Tolic studies Stefan with his magnifying glass.

"Their *chaman* knows your son,' I say. "Last month, when we brought the rattlesnake head to their village so he could bury it, he was fascinated by Stefan's hair."

Ivan arcs his eyebrows at me but translates anyway. The Bliatoks turn to me, wide-eyed. Too late, I remember that Stefan would never have told his parents about the Yanomani village. I glance at Stefan. Even he has the good sense to turn his face toward the wall and say nothing.

"We're...we're wasting time," I splutter. "I'm...I'm positive the medicine man can help him."

Tolic speaks up in his father's cosmopolitan German, in his best parent-pleasing, polite voice. "Frau and Herr Bliatok, I too, was on this heroic expedition to the Yanomani village. Their medicine man did take a liking to Stefan. He was fascinated with your son's blond hair. More than that, awestruck. Perhaps he'd never seen such golden hair before. I'm sure he will remember Stefan fondly, and do his very best to help your son."

We all watch the Bliatoks closely.

Once they got over the shock of hearing sophisticated *Berlin-Stil* German in the middle of the Venezuela jungle, they nod, in hope and understanding.

Señoría Bliatok says something to Ivan, who runs to the mayor's house. He and the mayor return with a bucket of ice, a blanket, leather umbrellas, and a stretcher.

A scowling Señor Bliatok, the mayor, Tolic, and I pull Stefan onto the stretcher. Señoría Bliatok packs ice around his neck and more in his armpits. She wraps ice in a washcloth and places it on his forehead.

Our mayor speaks only Spanish. "Don't worry, Señoría. We will take every precaution with your precious son. The Yanomani are fierce, but in their own way, they're fair."

Ivan translates. "This is madness," Señor Bliatok says.

It is still early morning as Tolic and I, and Señor Bliatok and the mayor, step onto the jungle trail with Stefan on a stretcher. We each hold a corner of the stretcher with one hand. The other holds a leather umbrella, as protection from the arrow snakes.

Myron and Zenon have distracted Dog. The Yanomani would want Dog's brilliant feathers for the chaman's necklace. And Dog for their dinner.

Our best jungle chopper, Señor Nicholas, walks well ahead of us. He brandishes his longest machete and cuts the trail wider toward the new Yanomani village.

Chapter Thirteen
The Circle Widens

As we stand in the outskirts of their village, the girls, women, and howler monkeys shriek. Tolic and I don't flinch because we expected this greeting. The men tremble in wide-eyed terror.

It is the same Yanomani men who greet us. I recognize their tattoos. Two men side wind their arms like rattlesnakes to show us that they remember us.

Stefan groans. He still radiates heat.

This is for Stefan, the miracle.

We all nod and smile at one another. The New Barcelona men gesture toward their fields and nod approvingly. The crops are bigger than they were even a month ago. All these men are farmers, I think suddenly. They all grow their family's food. We have that in common.

Women stir cook pots. Girls weave mats.

Small boys chase one another with sticks as spears. They glance our way expectantly, to see if we are watching them practice their hunting skills. Not one of us gives the boys an encouraging smile.

Meanwhile, Stefan's breath becomes weaker and weaker.

"Please good sirs, we need your *chaman*," Tolic says in his best parent-pleasing, polite voice. In Spanish this time, although it wouldn't matter in what language he speaks, come to think of it.

With a flourish, we pull the blanket off Stefan.

The Yanomani men frown and then speak to one another. A man who hooked his arm like a rattlesnake runs to the *shabono.*

The howler monkeys have stopped shrieking. There is no noise except the throbbing hum of thousands of insects, the bird song from the jungle canopy, and the distant roar of the jaguars.

The *chaman* runs toward us with a basket full of leaves, half gourds of water, and liquids and powders. He does remember Stefan, for he toys with his blond hair for a moment. The medicine man lifts Stefan's back off the stretcher; he pours a bright green liquid down his throat.

The men stare at Stefan. They expect something will happen, and soon. We men and boys of New Barcelona look at him, too.

"Do you feel differently, Stefan? Do you feel any better?" I ask him.

"Pedrito, it's much too soon for a cure," Señor Mr. Bliatok says. "I still say this is madness."

Heat still rolls of Stefan, as though I am standing too close to Mama's stove on the hottest summer day.

Suddenly, Stephan groans. He rolls off the stretcher and kneels on the ground. On his hands and knees, Stefan throws up, again and again. The Yanomani *chaman* nods to his fellow tribesmen. They nod back.

Stefan can't stop throwing up. It's as though the green liquid is scraping the sickness right out of his body. After many minutes, he stops. The vomiting makes his fever peak. Stefan glows like white-hot charcoal.

The medicine man gives him another medicine—an orange liquid this time—and two gourdfuls of water. After about fifteen minutes, Stefan blinks as though returning from a faraway place.

"Papa," Stefan says, panting. His face blooms fiery red. We all cheer as the tell-tale sweat runs down his forehead.

"Stefan," his father says softly as he touches his son's face. "Your fever has broken. You're hot, but no longer dry hot." Señor Bliatok looks at the *chaman.* "What did you give him, to make his fever break so fast?"

Stefan looks around him. "Papa, why am I in the Yanomani village? Has Pedrito killed another rattlesnake?"

"No, son." Stefan's father sobs. "This man gave you an emetic, to make you vomit. He gave you something else…your fever broke so fast. 've never seen anything like it."

Stefan points to the bucket. "Is that ice for eating?" he asks in Spanish.

"Have all the ice you want, Stefan." The mayor gives him the bucket. "There's plenty here, and plenty more at my house."

Stefan chews ice as though it were Christmas candy.

Stefan's father sobs in his hands. The *chaman* and the rest of the Yanomani don't look surprised to see Stefan recovering so quickly.

I was right—they did know exactly what was wrong, some sort of Amazonian sickness that they've treated for years and years.

"They knew what was wrong with you," I say. "They knew."

"You were right, Pedrito, and I was wrong," Señor Bliatok says as he dries his eyes. "Whatever was wrong with my son, surely no doctor in Minsk has ever seen it. I brought money. I must pay the doctor."

Stefan's father stands up and digs into his pants pocket. He holds Venezuelan currency out to the medicine man. The *chaman* frowns.

"No, no," Stefan's father says. "We don't take charity. We pay our way."

He places the money in the *chaman*'s palm. The paper currency, with Simon Bolivar's stern portrait printed on it, drifts to the ground like dried leaves.

"Money means nothing to them," I say.

"I have American dollars at home." Stefan's father turns to me. "Tell the Señor Doctor, I have twenty American dollars at home."

I shrug. "American money will mean nothing to them as well. We…we don't have anything to give them. Nothing they'd want."

"I have something," Tolic calls out in Spanish. "Look what I can do."

Tolic holds his magnifying glass a few inches from a leaf. An intense bolt of sunlight concentrates on the bright green surface. Like magic, it smolders before bursting into flames.

The men cry out. Tolic gives the magnifying glass to the *chaman*.

The *chaman* plucks a leaf from a bush and points the magnifying glass toward it. Nothing happens.

Tolic shakes his head and points to the sun. He guides the *chaman*'s hand, to hold the magnifying glass in precisely the right way, so the sun rays merge onto another plucked leaf. I point to the white-hot bolt of sunlight. The leaf smolders before it bursts into flames.

The medicine man tries it. He holds the magnifying glass to create a concentrated beam of sunlight on another leaf. The leaf smolders; a tiny flame bursts from the surface.

The *chaman* laughs. He tries another leaf and another. He drops them to his feet as they each catch fire and burn.

I say, "Tolic, you've given them exactly what they need. They can start fires for cooking food, for boiling water."

Tolic points to the magnifying glass. He then bows low, as though he were in the presence of a member of a European royal family—a Borbón, a

Hapsburg, a Horslev, or a Romanov. The *chaman* smiles. The men who greeted us touch the magnifying glass gingerly, as though it were a magical thing.

Stefan's father stuffs the paper currency into his pockets. "Stefan, lie down on the stretcher."

"I can walk back to New Barcelona," Stefan says. "I'm fine."

"Your fever may have broken but you're still sick," Señor Bliatok argues back. "Lie down."

"I'm fine," Stefan insists.

"We need to leave," the mayor says as he eyes a row of spears, lined up against a rail like the uprights to a fence. Each spear-tip glistens with poisoned beeswax.

"I'll roll up the stretcher. No sudden movements, Señor Nicholas says softly. "If Stefan needs it, we'll set it up in the jungle." He too, is eyeing the spears. "*Vamanos*."

We pick up our leather umbrellas, nodding and smiling as before.

But the Yanomani are paying no attention to us. The medicine man is starting small fires, as their women clap in delight. Yanomani children dip their fingers in the ice bucket and cry out as the melting ice burns their fingers.

Fire and ice—always different and always the same.

The magnifying glass…it's a circle.

I gasp. "Señor Gutiérrez is wrong. A circle isn't strongest when it's closed." The DP's give me puzzled looks. "It's when a circle is open."

It may take the power of Superman to smash open a circle Bang! Pow! Punch! But it takes a different kind of courage to keep it open. "We'll be fine, I say with the same conviction that I feel. "They won't hurt us. We're in their circle now."

As we leave the village, the howler monkeys begin to shriek.

Halfway home, Stefan does need to lie down on the stretcher.

Chapter Fourteen

A Blooming Flower

When we return home, I see something I've never seen before. My parents are folk dancing together in the village commons. Dancing?

Mama has her hands on her waist. She steps and kicks her feet in an intricate and complicated dance. Her ankles pump up and down. I've never seen her dance before. These steps must be from her childhood.

Papa is dancing, too, the same intricate steps. He lifts her off her feet and they spin. Mama is laughing as her skirt sweeps into a circle. She looks like a blooming flower.

Myron and Zenon are skipping in circles but in a half-hearted way, as though uncertain of why Mama and Papa are so happy. Dog is running in circles, too. He must think they are all playing a game with him.

"Papa?"

My father stops dancing. "Our visas have finally come through. We're going to America!"

"America?"

Papa waves some papers in front of my nose. "We're going to America at last! The mayor had a certified letter delivered to his house. But my name was on the envelope! It's our letter. It's our visas."

"America?"

"Here is the best part. Your mother and I have been saving money for years to pay for the journey, but a Methodist Mission in a place called Cleveland has bought our airline tickets to New York City, and our railroad tickets to Cleveland. This means we'll have money to spend when we arrive."

Papa lifts Mama off her feet again.

Mama is laughing. "The Statue of Liberty!"

Papa says in return, "The Empire State building!"

"Where will we live, Papa?"

He sets Mama down. "This place." Papa points to a paragraph. "It's called Cleveland, Ohio. Someone from the Mission will meet us at the airport. They say there are lots of Eastern Europeans in Northeast Ohio. We'll feel right at home."

"Ohio." This is the place where President Rutherford B. Hayes was born. "Are there many South Americans in Ohio?"

"Who cares? We're North Americans now."

"Promise me, Karol," Mama says. "Promise me that Cleveland, Ohio, is not a cold place."

"Oh, no, no, Katrina." Papa waves his hand airily. "They would never send us to a cold place."

DP's are looking out of their Quonset huts at my family; the lucky Buczkowskis have gotten their visas at last. Ivan, Maria, Elizabeth, and all their brothers and sisters—they all stare at us in grim, sullen envy. Tolic has crossed the Zimmer's bridge and has not heard the news, not yet.

Only Dog is paying no attention. He claws at the dirt and swallows a beetle whole. Bwarf.

What about Dog?

"Papa, we can take Dog with us to America, can't we?"

Papa hasn't heard me. He is lifting Mama by her waist again. Her right hand is on Papa's shoulder, the other is high over her head. Her back is an arched bow, a half moon, as her pointed toes and left arm reach back.

Mama's skirt is like a blooming flower once more, as she laughs and laughs at the sky.

Chapter Fifteen

Best Friends Forever

"Anatole will give Dog a good home," Papa says. He's been repeating the same sentence for days.

Our breakfast rice and eggs are steaming. My parents have already lifted their glasses to toast their survival. To their survival—Myron, Zenon, and I are doing just fine, right here in Venezuela.

"He's your friend," Mama repeats for the umpteenth time. "He's known Dog since he was a chick. He was right here when Dog hatched."

"No, he wasn't," I repeat for the umpteenth time. "Tolic flew to Rio de Janeiro for Christmas. Dog hatched on Christmas Eve afternoon. I remember."

My parents have stopped listening to me, to Myron, to Zenon. All they can talk about it is leaving

Venezuela and going to America. To Mama and Papa, New Barcelona is a spot to mark time, to wait for something better to come along. For all these years, their real home has been the United States of America. Mama and Papa really are Delayed Pilgrims.

"How far is Washington from New York? Mama asks Papa.

"Not far at all," Papa says, as though he is an expert.

"Not far at all." Mama repeats. "That means our sons will see their capital city someday."

"Katrina, you mean our capital. We're going to America. Our dream, Katrina. " Papa has tears in his eyes.

Mama frets as she picks up her fork. "All our clothes are twenty years old. "We'll walk down the streets of Manhattan looking like extras from *Top Hat.* From a Fred Astaire movie…from…from years ago."

"We'll buy new clothes, Katrina," Papa says. "Anything you want."

"For years I looked like an orphan and now I look like a refugee. I want us to look like Americans…"

"Anything you want, Katrina. We're starting our new life at last."

"…like prosperous, settled Americans."

"Anything you want."

Until Papa got our visas, our entire day, our every day, was set: from gathering eggs at dawn to watching Dog settle in for the night. In between, the Buczkowskis lived in a comforting routine, as comforting as Venezuelan hot chocolate, as comforting as the daily soccer match in the village commons, as comforting as the annual President Rutherford B. Hayes essay contest.

I may have thought of myself as a Delayed Pilgrim but now that we're leaving, actually leaving, I know that I haven't been waiting to leave. I'm not waiting for anything.

I live here. Home is Venezuela.

Papa and Mama don't even look at us anymore. Now they're talking about the New York Central Railroad, which will take us from New York City to Cleveland, by way of Pennsylvania.

"Pennsylvania," I say. "That's where our Christmas Hershey bars come from, right Papa?"

Papa is talking about the train going through a mountain range called the Alleghenies. "Pennsylvanians built tunnels going right through the mountains. It's as dark as night in the train compartments."

"Will we fall asleep in the tunnels, Mama?" Zenon asks.

I feel like…what? Like I'm in the middle of the Orinoco River at flood stage, and the river is rushing forward much too fast, and I'm caught up in it.

"The tunnels are short," Myron answers. "They can't be more than a mile or two long, right Papa? We won't fall asleep."

I say, "Tolic wants to show me the chicken coop he's had built." My feet can't find the river bottom and I'm tumbling forward….

"Anatole will take good care of Dog," Papa says.

"He's your friend," Mama says. "Tolic was right here when Dog hatched. He's known Dog since he was a chick."

I start to explain again about Tolic in Rio de Janerio for Christmas but I stop. Why bother?

Pan American Airlines allows real dogs on their flights, and cats, but no other animals. Papa went to the mayor's house and spoke into a telephone. This is what the Pan American Airlines employee told him.

"The Zimmers have invited the Buczkowskis for lunch, remember? All of us are invited."

Mama looks up from her eggs. "All of us?"

Papa stares at me. "All of us?"

"Why didn't you tell me sooner?" Mama scolds. "I need to wash my hair, iron my best dress."

"I DID tell you. I told you THREE DAYS ago. You and Papa were talking about the ferry to the Statue of Liberty. You don't LISTEN anymore."

Silence.

I wait for Papa to scold me, how that's no way to speak to your mother. How I should apologize to her this instant.

Instead, he apologizes to me. "I'm sorry, Pedrito. But you need to understand: your mother and I have dreamt of going to America for a long time, long before we were married, long before you or your brothers were born. It was our dream, a dream born in the potato slave camps. Our dream sustained us through horror you can't imagine.

"It was our dream that kept us alive. Isn't that right, Katrina?"

Mama has already left the table. She is laying out her best dress and hat on her bed. Even I know this close-fitting, beige silk dress with padded shoulders was the fashion twenty years ago. All the American actresses in the movie magazines wear full skirts, fluffy sweaters, and little scarves tied around their necks.

Whatever fashionable ladies wore in 1938 Berlin…well, it's a safe bet Methodists ladies didn't wear the same in Oklahoma City. Tolic's mother will know Mama's best dress is a shabby hand-me-down. In the middle of all the Zimmer's *opulencia,* Mama will look like a refugee, the wretched refuse, a Displaced Person, someone nobody else wants.

For the first time in my life I pity Mama. My pity feels as prickly hot as an itchy wool blanket. She deserves more than what Venezuela has offered her. Mama was just a bit older than me, when she became a potato slave. Doesn't she deserve stylish clothes from a fancy dress shop in New York City?

Don't I deserve to widen my circle? New York City…the Statute of Liberty…a new school in Ohio as big as our village…beef, chicken, and Pepsi-Cola every day…a change in the weather….

The Nazis will only call the tune if I let them. I just won't let them. In America, those *Niemskie swinie* won't grunt, wallow in the mud, and smirk at the Buczkowskis anymore.

"How will I look?" Mama holds the dress up to her shoulders. The matching hat is perched on her head--fake cherries on the brim and a tiny veil that hangs across her forehead. "I'll go to the mayor's house and borrow his wife's iron."

"You'll look beautiful, Katrina," Papa says, "quite the lady."

"I've never been to an elegant lunch party before," Mama says. Her eyes are shining. "I have a thousand things to do. Karol, wear the blue suit. I'll brush it when I return.

"Pedrito, you're in charge of your brothers. Get the shirts out of the clothes crate, the button-down shirts. You're old enough to wear a tie."

I choke on my egg. "A tie?"

"We'll all look our best. We'll wear the same clothes on the airplane."

"Mama—a necktie?"

"I have a thousand things to do," she says happily.

Three hours later, the Buczkowskis are clean and dressed in their best clothes. Myron, Zenon, and I are wearing dark blue shorts with light blue button-down shirts. Even Zenon is wearing a tie, which he tugs at whenever Mama isn't looking. Papa is wearing his blue wool suit.

Mama looks beautiful. Even Papa stares at her in astonishment. The mayor's wife lent her a pair of brown high heels with a matching belt and purse. She lent Mama a pretty straw sunhat with a blue ribbon on the brim. Mama is wearing lipstick and rouge. Her eyes sparkle.

As usual, Dog follows me.

"Katrina," Papa says sternly. "You do understand about the Zimmers, don't you? They're DPs just as we are."

I turn to watch Mama, for I have been worried about this, too. What if she screams about rich Nazis and potato slaves? What if the Zimmers ask her to leave, and Dog doesn't have a home after all? Mama has never been to Tolic's. She's never looked across his family's bridge. She has no idea of the *opulencia* she's about to see.

"Of course I understand," Mama snaps. "The Zimmers fled Hitler's Nazis before the Germans invaded Poland. It's not a matter of forgiveness for there is nothing to forgive. Pedrito has explained everything."

Yes, I have explained everything to her, time and time again. But only since letting Dog into her life she has forgiven the Zimmers, and forgiven the world: the clear weather and the endless sky.

She pats my father's arm. "Let's enjoy our lunch. We're going to America. There's nothing to forgive. "

"Pedrito's circles, Mama," Myron says.

I punch Myron on the arm and hope Mama isn't listening. Just my luck: she's all ears this time. "Your circles?"

"In geometry class, Señor Gutiérrez said circles are strongest when they're closed. We think that's good, they're supposed to be closed. But when we open them…good things come in and bad things tumble out. It's silly."

Mama adjusts her hat. "No it isn't. A circle is strongest when it's closed, true enough, but think of all it is missing—poor, lonely circle."

Our lunch: fresh fruit from Chile, cold shrimp salad, smoked salmon from Nova Scotia, tiny *cachapas*, although Frau Zimmer calls the tiny pancakes blintzes, cold herring in sour cream, and two cakes for dessert with big scoops of vanilla ice cream to go with the cakes.

Tolic, my brothers and I drink lemonade. Our parents drink something called mimosas—orange juice and champagne.

The Zimmer's dining room is as big as our house. To keep us cool, a ceiling fan rotates high above our heads.

Servants keep bringing food out from the kitchen. We boys keep our heads down and eat, and eat. Our parents talk as old friends.

In Mama's Polish and Frau Zimmer's German, the mothers talk about schools in the United States.

In German, Papa and Herr Zimmer talk about automobiles.

Papa stands up. “I’d like to talk about Dog,” he says in German, looking right at me, “so the Zimmers understand what a very special bird he is. We’ve guessed that Dog is an araucana. Chinese explorers traveled to what is now Chile, centuries before Columbus. They brought chickens with them. The araucana hens are large, true enough, but it’s the roosters that are huge.

“He’s a keen predator, Anatole, so be sure he has lots of insects in his cage. He’ll want to chase and catch them. It’s in his nature.”

Tolic smiles. “*O--kay*, Señor Buczkowski.”

Papa smiles back. “*O--kay*. This has been a wonderful lunch, but we have to pack. The mayor is driving us to Caracas before dawn.”

Mama stands up. “Thank you so much for your hospitality. Anatole has been such a good friend to Pedrito.”

Herr Zimmer and Frau Zimmer stand up. “You’re very welcome,” Herr Zimmer says in passable Polish. “Anatole crosses the bridge to home, and it’s all he can talk about at the dinner table—his adventures with Pedrito.”

“I’m sure Pedrito wants to see Dog,” Tolic says.

In the deep shade next to the Zimmer's sun porch is a pen built just for Dog. Carpenters have built it special and it's twice the size of our chicken coop. They used a heavy chicken wire from Manhattan, Kansas. The roof is the same shining copper of the Zimmer's house.

A man will stand guard at night to keep Dog safe.

Dog is already in the pen. He comes up to me, pushes his head right through the wire. As I stroke the feathers just under his beak, his brilliant colors blur into a bright, puddled swirl. Tolic is standing next to me.

I say, "He likes to be petted, right here under his beak."

It's hard to talk all of a sudden.

"You'll never forget Dog," Tolic says. He looks down as I wipe tears away.

"I'll send you photographs. Send me your address when you get to…to…"

"Ohio," I choke out. "This isn't the last time I'll see you."

Tolic says. "I'll visit you." He is crying now, too. It's my turn to look down.

My brothers stand to my left. "Dog, *mi hermanito,"* Zenon howls.

Tolic says, "Joe Shuster and Jerry Siegel, Pedrito. Two Jewish kids from Cleveland created Superman. We'll visit them. We'll find their addresses in the phone book. We'll trade comic books with them. It'll be fun."

Papa puts his hand on my head. "It's time to go."

I sniff, hard. "Is that true, Papa? Superman is from Cleveland?"

"Isn't he from the Planet Krypton?" Papa asks.

"The boys who created Superman live in Cleveland, Señor Buczkowski," Tolic explains. He doesn't understand that Papa was teasing. "When I visit you, we could visit them, too."

"Anatole, that's a wonderful idea," Papa says.

Tolic touches my arm. "*Mejores amigos para siempre*."

I try to say it back but I'm crying too hard: Best friends forever.

Bwarf. Bwarf.

If Dog can say it so can I. "*Mejores. Amigos. Para. Siempre*." I say between gasps. I throw my arms around Tolic's shoulders.

Mama must have been listening. She speaks to Dog softly as she pets him just under his beak.

On the way home, Papa says, "Pedrito, the first Superman comic book was printed twenty years ago, when I was your age. They're grown men, like me."

"Oh." I can't keep the disappoint from my voice.

"But we'll visit them," Papa says quickly. "When we open a circle, good things enter in."

"Let's be Douglas DC-Sevens," Myron says.

Zenon runs forward. "Grummm, grumm."

My brothers raise their arms as wings. As they run, they look like huge birds lifting themselves up in ever-widening circles, up toward the sky.

"Tomorrow's my birthday," I say. "I'll be thirteen."

Chapter Sixteen
Window Seat

We're in the Caracas airport and my brothers are crying.

It's just before dawn, and all around us are people, people who work for the airport, people who work for the airlines, and people who are flying today. I've never seen so many people all at once in my life. They flow around us like Orinoco River water over rocks.

Papa has to shout to be heard above the sobbing. "Today is Pedrito's birthday. He gets to sit in the window seat."

Zenon sniffs loudly. Myron scowls.

At the airline desk, the mayor shows me how to ask for our tickets. He tells me to tell my parents good luck, and good travels. We follow the passengers outside and climb a steep staircase into the airplane.

The stewardess has to show us how to fasten our seat belts.

The plane moves forward. I'm in an airplane! My heart is pounding as the plane turns a sharp left for the runway. It's a high-pitched whine, like giant mosquitoes flying around my ears. As the plane lifts, I feel slammed against my seat. As the plane lifts more, the airport looks like toy buildings scattered across a dirt floor.

"Thrust," Papa shouts above the noise. Myron is sitting next to me and Papa is sitting on his right. Mama and Zenon are in the seats across the aisle.

"Thrust is the high speed of the plane, pushing against you."

Zenon howls again.

As we ascend, all I see is rain forest and ocean. From the air, Venezuela looks like dense jungle and nothing more. The Yanomani, the Venezuelans, and the Displaced Persons, my friends, all the animals, Dog have .... disappeared under the tree canopy, as if they were never there.

Will I ever return? Will I ever see Dog and my friends again? Will Stefan get better? If Stefan, Ivan, and Tolic get visas, where will they go?

My ears are blocked, as though something is stuffed all the way into them. Zenon's mouth is open but the screaming is muffled. I point to my ears and Myron nods and smiles. He can't hear Zenon much, either.

Last night, Papa said South America is much further east than North America. For hours, all I see is cloudless sky and endless ocean in broad streaks of green and blue.

For lunch, the stewardess gives us hot chicken, rice, vegetables, and chocolate cake on a metal tray. My brothers and I each receive a small glass bottle with cold milk in it. The cold milk and the warm chocolate cake are delicious together.

All that swallowing finally opens my ears. All of a sudden, passengers are shouting at one another above the roar of the airplane.

Gradually, our pilot bows left. "I see it!" I shout. "Land! The United States of America!" Everyone crowds the windows. The pilot orders the passengers to return to their seats.

I'm already in my seat, and I see it all, my birthday present.

Sparkling white yachts plow through the deep-blue Atlantic. We fly further east. The Washington Monument pops into the distance.

Papa takes us all to the toilet. One by one, he shows us how to use it. After Zenon flushes, he runs to the nearest window. "Where did all the blue water go?" he asks.

"Time to sit down," Papa says, as he rushes us back to our seats. We fasten our seatbelts with sharp *clicks.*

Our pilot says we're going to land shortly. He announces New York City to our left, and I see it all. Manhattan Island is crowded with buildings, each one taller than the next. Why doesn't the island sink under all that weight? I want to ask Papa why, but I don't want people to laugh at me.

The Statue of Liberty! She faces serenely outward toward Europe, because that's where immigrants to America came from first.

Mama is crying. "I see her," she shouts. "I see her."

Even Papa has tears in his eyes.

The pilot welcomes us to the United States of America, and the Idlewild Airport of New York City. Everyone cheers.

The plane lands with a bump I feel in my bones. As the engines wind down, the great roaring noise I've gotten used to ends. The sudden quiet is like sundown, when all the jungle birds stop singing, squawking, cawing and tuck in for the night.

We follow the crowd to something called 'baggage claim.' Luggage falls out of a shoot and lands with a *thud* on a silver-y wheel that keeps turning, turning.... Like magic, our three suitcases appear. Papa grabs them as other passengers grab theirs.

Papa must see my baffled stare. "The luggage was in the belly of the plane. Someone put the luggage in the belly in Caracas, and someone else pulled it out again here in New York City."

Papa looks around. "Someone from the Mission is supposed to meet us."

A man is holding up a sign that says:

Buczkowski

"Is that man the President of the United States?" Zenon asks.

"Shush," Mama says.

Papa extends his hand and immediately the man starts to speak Spanish. He greets our family and explains about the Mission. We'll be here for two days before taking the train to Cleveland.

The man keeps talking, "the Buczkowski family will see the sights of Manhattan. I will be your guide."

My brothers and I smile and nod. Two days with no school, no egg gathering, no water carrying, no cutting down jungle, no vegetable harvests…

Meanwhile, my parents are as lost as they were in New Barcelona. "Pedrito," Papa says, "tell this man we were hoping for a guide who speaks Polish. Surely there're people in New York City who speak Polish."

After I ask him, our guide is dumbfounded. "A family from Venezuela wants a guide who speaks Polish?"

"My parents are from Poland. What's your name, Señor?"

"The war. Of course, so sad. Tell your parents I'll see want I can do. I am Mr. Lobos. We'll go through customs, and then I'll take you to the taxi stand and to your hotel. Welcome to the United States of America."

Mama insists on holding Zenon's hand on the left and Myron's hand on the right as we navigate through crowds of people. White, black, brown, yellow—every sort of person I can think of is trotting through the airport. Hurry, hurry, hurry. What's the rush?

At customs, Mr. Lobos explains to a Spanish-speaking American man in a gray uniform that we are poor refugees, Displaced Persons from WWII. He waves us through with a smile.

Our taxi driver helps us load our suitcases into the trunk. Mr. Lobos keeps talking, "Venezue-la time is thirty minutes ahead of Eastern Daylight Savings Time." He pats his wrist. "Set your watches."

Papa and Mama give him baffled stares. Papa looks at his wrist, as though expecting to see something new there. "We don't have wristwatches," I tell our guide. "Those three suitcases in the trunk are all we have."

"Ah. I had nothing when I came here," Mr. Lobos says, "poorer than your family is right now. 'Blessed are you poor, for yours is the kingdom of God.' "

After I translate, Papa looks sad.

"Luke 6:20." Mr. Lobos smiles at us.

"Tell Mr. Lobos I know that verse," Papa says. The taxi picks up speed as we drive over bridges and through tunnels.

Mr. Lobos says, "We're here. Welcome to midtown Manhattan."

The Buczkowskis step onto the sidewalk. Zenon claps his hands over his ears and howls. Noise assaults us. It's the roar of thousands of engines from cars, trucks, buses. Car and truck horns blare.

New York City is even louder than the airplane.

The sidewalk shakes below our feet. An earthquake?

"The subway!" Mr. Lobos shouts. "You'll get used to the noise!"

Manhattan smells like hot engines and gasoline, like a pile of burning rubber trees. Gray clouds blanket the streets. My eyes sting.

"Air pollution!" Mr. Lobos shouts. "You'll get used to it. Try not to take deep breaths when you're outside. You'll be fine. Let's keep moving."

As we stand in the hotel, we all start to shiver. "The lobby is air conditioned," Mr. Lobos says, "a steady seventy-five degrees and low humidity. Perfect air."

We glance uneasily at Mama. The cold. But she is paying no attention. Instead, she's staring at the women in fashionable dresses and hats. She studies their shoes and handbags.

A man in a uniform loads our luggage onto a wagon.

"He's the bell-hop," Mr. Lobos says. "And here's the elevator."

We step into a tiny room with no windows. Our guide pushes a numbered light while an old man in another uniform glares at him.

"I forgot. It's his job to push the buttons." Mr. Lobos shrugs at the old man. The old man scowls.

So many different jobs! There's pushing buttons, hauling luggage, driving taxis, flying airplanes, and standing behind customs and reservation desks. Each job has its own uniform. Surely Papa can find some sort of job here in America.

Zenon howls in terror as the tiny room goes up and up. Myron and I push into the corners. Myron howls in terror, too, and my heart throbs in my throat.

"Boys, shush," Mama says, "I haven't been in an elevator since I was a girl. The department stores in Warsaw all had them."

Our guide looks at her politely but with no understanding on his face. The tiny room keeps lifting up. "I'm from Cuba," he says to me.

The old man in the uniform pushes a button. Like magic, the elevator door opens.

"Let's keep moving." Mr. Lobos walks us down the hallway and then gives Papa what looks like a tiny knife.

"It's a key." Papa laughs. "I haven't seen a key since the Nazis invaded Poland." He puts the key in a narrow hole in the door and fumbles a bit. The door opens.

Our hotel room has two huge beds. My brothers rush into our own bathroom. “Look!” Myron shouts. “Running water, just like at the mayor’s house. I can blend them to make warm water, as warm as I want it.”

Immediately, Zenon flushes the toilet. “It doesn’t stink!” he shrieks.

Mr. Lobos grins at us.

“We not used to indoor plumbing,” I say.

“Neither was I when I first came here. It will take a few months to get used to everything. I’ve been in New York City for two years. The rest of it,” here our guide points vaguely west, ‘that’s the state, New York State--”

“Where does the water go?” Zenon interrupts.

Mr. Lobos says, “Oh, under the building. Pipes.”

“Where does it go after that?” Myron asks.

“I…I don’t know.” He shrugs. “Tell your parents I’ll meet them in the restaurant downstairs in thirty minutes. You must be hungry.”

Mama sits on one of the beds. I’ve never
seen the dark splotches under her eyes before. “I’m exhausted.”

Papa says, “Pedrito, tell our guide we’ll stay
here.”

Mr. Lobos says, “I’ll take the boys

downstairs. Your parents can order room service." He must see the baffled look on my face. "It means the hotel staff will serve them right here in the room." Someone knocks on our door. "There's the bell-hop with your luggage."

I translate once again. Mama nods. "I remember room service. All the fashionable hotels in Warsaw had it."

We take the elevator downstairs. Without Mama to cling to, Zenon hangs on to my right arm. Myron hangs on to my left. I have no one to hang on to.

"We won't fall," I say above a fresh wave of howls.

"What keeps us from falling?" Myron's voice is shaking.

"I don't know." Mr. Lobos glances uneasily at the ceiling.

"*No hay problema, Manitos,*" another bell hop on the elevator tells us, "*la electridad.*"

"See?" Mr. Lobos is all smiles. "It's all electric. You have nothing to worry about."

When the door opens my brothers and I rush out into the lobby.

In the restaurant, Myron holds up a bottle of red sauce. "What's this?"

"Ketchup," Mr. Lobos says. "A tomato

sauce, Americans put it on everything."

A woman in a uniform brings us our food.

"Here we are. Hamburgers and French fries," Mr. Lobos says.

"These French fries are potatoes. Are they all the way from France?" Myron asks.

"You're asking too many questions," I say to my brother in Polish. "Our guide is becoming irritated."

Myron shouts back in Polish, "A thousand pardons."

Mr. Lobos sputters into his coffee and cream. "What?"

We dig in. A hamburger tastes good with ketchup on it. So do the fried potatoes. My brothers and I drink iced Pepsi-Cola. With ice, it's much colder than when we drink it on Saturdays with Food Feast. It's even colder than when Tolic and I drank it on the way to Angel Falls. Delicious.

I feel the cold, all the way down my throat and into my stomach.

We all have chocolate ice cream in small metal cups for dessert.

Myron says, "Chocolate for the second time in the same day. Do Americans eat chocolate twice a day?"

I kick his ankle under the table. "Too many questions."

Mr. Lobos wastes no time leading us up the staircase. "Tomorrow at nine o'clock. Good night." He almost runs to the elevator.

Our parents are eating their dinners on a tray.

"Look," Papa says.

The television is on. We watch, fascinated, as people in the television look right at us. The women in the television are holding soap and toothpaste. The men are dressed as cowboys. They're holding cigarettes.

Suddenly, the picture changes to Superman. Superman in the television! Unlike the comic books Tolic lets me borrow, this Superman is not in color. Everything—Superman, the phone booth Clark Kent changes in, the buildings, the rockets—everything is in shades of gray.

We all listen closely. Zenon and Myron look at me expectantly for the translation, since I read them Tolic's Superman comic books.

"What are they saying, Pedrito?" Zenon asks.

I understand nothing anyone is saying. Not even Superman is making any sense and I could always understand him when I read the comic books.

"Why can't I understand what they're saying? I can read English."

"You're not used to hearing the spoken language," Papa says. "You'll get it. The secret is to listen closely. One moment you'll realize that you've understood a word, then a sentence, then a conversation. It'll happen."

I point to a man who's as bald as an egg. "He's the bad guy," I bluff. "Superman wants to stop him from taking over the world."

Myron scoffs. "All the bad guys want to take over the world, Pedrito. You don't know what's going on any more than I do."

Superman is flying. He's flying! His cape is flapping. His arms are outstretched. His feet are gliding the air. The music swells....

A man appears on the television dressed as a sea captain. He's holding the ship's wheel. Outside it's storming, rain is coming down in sheets as the ship is tossed from side to side. The sea captain lights a cigarette.

Like magic, the storm ends.

The sea captain winks at us and holds the pack of cigarettes up to the screen so we can see the brand. The sea captain says, "Chesterfields."

"That means it's time to go to bed," Papa says. "It's been a long day."

Mama is already asleep. Zenon, Myron, and I share the second bed, just like back home in New Barcelona.

Sleep. I've always wanted to notice the moment my brain switches from awake to asleep but I've never felt it before.

After my first day in America, I feel it.

Awake.

Switch; like magic.

Asleep.

Chapter Seventeen

Extra Credit

At exactly nine o'clock the next morning, a courteous knock on the door wakes us up. "Mr. Lobos," I say as I open it.

He greets us with a polite frown. "The hotel restaurant stops serving breakfast at nine-thirty. You'll have to hurry."

"Papa, the breakfast time is almost over," Myron shouts.

Mama sits up. "I'll have the room service again. Pedrito, tell Mr. Lobos to have my breakfast sent up here."

"They'll be none of that," Papa says sharply. "Room service costs extra. We can't impose on the Methodists."

"I can't leave our room—"

"We don't live in the Emporia Hotel in New York City. Get dressed."

Mr. Lobos has been watching us politely. He had to have heard my father's angry voice. I explain, "My mother doesn't like going from a familiar place to an unfamiliar place."

Mr. Lobos shrugs. "She should recite something in her head to take her mind off going into the unknown. Here she feels safe. Outside is the unknown."

"How do you know that?" I ask. She's sitting in a chair in the corner and clutching the armrests so hard her knuckles are white.

"I was a student in Cuba, learning to be a psychologist. There's going to be a revolution in Cuba. We got out just in time."

"What's he talking about?" Papa asks. "A revolution? Here?"

"No, it's--" I'm already getting tired of translating back and forth, back and forth. I switch to Polish. "We need to go downstairs, Mama. Mr. Lobos says there's no room service for breakfast." I take a deep breath. This will be such a mean thing to say, but we can't leave Mama here. "I know you don't want to go hungry."

A look of terror crosses her face, as a cloud shadows the sun.

Quickly, we get dressed. Papa pushes and we pull to get Mama over the threshold. We pay no attention to her moans. The elevator again but this Zenon doesn't howl.

"You're no longer afraid of the elevator," I tell him. "Good for you."

Zenon spins in a circle. "I'm pretending it's a rocket. I'm a rocket man."

"You should spin, too," I say to Myron.

"So should you," Myron snaps. "You were as scared as I was."

At the restaurant, Mr. Lobos asks me, "What would you like to do today?
There's Central Park, and the Central Park Zoo. Every animal you could think of."

Zenon says, "the Zoo."

"A park is like a jungle," Mama says in a shaking voice. "Karol, you know I can't go into the jungle."

Papa says, "Central Park is like the Lazienski Park in Warsaw. Do you remember the Chopin Monument? Central Park is beautiful."

After breakfast, Papa takes Mama's arm as we step into the taxi. He takes her arm again as we step out into Central Park.

Mama is panting. "I need to sit down on that bench…"

"They'll be none of that!" Papa shouts. "Don't pull your family down with you, Katrina. This is our new beginning, our second chance. Don't ruin America for the boys."

Mama's eyes fill with tears. I remember what Mr. Lobos said.

"Mama, do you have anything memorized?"

She thinks for a moment. "When I was at school, I had to memorize each nation in Europe and their capital cities, with extra credit in English."

"Mr. Lobos says to recite something when you're about to do something that scares you."

"The lions and tigers, the lions and tigers," Zenon hops up and down.

Mr. Lobos points. "The big cats are over there."

Mama takes a deep breath. "St… st …Stockholm, Sweden. Cope…Cope …Copenhagen, Denmark, Oh…oh...Oslo, Norway…."

Mr. Lobos winks at me as Mama staggers to the big cat exhibit. She mutters capital cities and nations under her breath as we walk to the monkey house, the seal tank, and penguin pool.

Mama flatly refuses to go to the snake house. She opens her mouth to scream....

"Let's have lunch," Mr. Lobos says tactfully. "There's an automat around the corner. The automat is something brand new. It's a new way to eat."

The automat—it's a building with tall, multi-windowed machines with food inside. We decide what we want to eat. Mr. Lobos shows us how to put money in the machines and how to punch the correct button. All we have to do is take the food out of the windowed slot and find a table for six.

It's the middle of the afternoon and we're hungry. We choose roast beef sandwiches, potato salad, and milk. The windows open, like magic. Zenon howls for a slice of chocolate cake with whipped cream and cherries on top. He punches the right button but the cake stays put behind the window.

Myron asks, "Aren't we supposed to have chocolate twice a day?"

My stomach rumbles and I burp for the fifth time since breakfast. All this beef and potatoes is making my stomach feel peculiar. I'm used to rice, eggs, and vegetables.

Mama has her wits about her once again. "Zenon and Myron, stop fussing or I'll take you back to the hotel. Let's sit down. Who can say the names of the animals? In English? Mr. Lobos will be our judge."

I translate, and in careful English, we recite the words for the animals in the zoo: lions; tigers; a Rocky Mountain cougar; a Venezuelan jaguar; African gorillas; chimpanzees; spider monkeys; bears; California gray seals.

Mr. Lobos helps us with our pronunciation as our parents smile proudly.

I switch to Spanish. "There are a lot of alligators in the reptile house."

"There's an interesting story, and I'm not sure it's true." Mr. Lobos sips his coffee with cream. He sure drinks a lot of coffee. It must be a Cuban custom. "Children in the City go to Florida for vacations. They return with baby alligators for pets. Once the baby alligators become too big for the family bathtub, the children set them free into the sewers. That's the water under the buildings. Sometimes the alligators creep out of the sewers and find their way onto the sidewalks."

Myron's eyes widen.

"So, the Central Park Zoo has a policy. Exotic animals will be adopted by the Zoo, never any questions. What shall we see next?"

"The Empire State building," Myron says.

Papa mutters something to Mama.

"I'm very tired," she says. "I'd like to go back to the hotel."

Mr. Lobos leans back in his chair and studies Mama as though she's a patient. "I'm guessing she wants to return to the hotel? It's familiar?"

I nod.

"This has been a big day. It's no wonder your mother is exhausted. Tell your father I will take you and your brothers to the Empire State building. We'll be home in time for a late dinner."

Zenon's right cheek is flat against the table. He's fast asleep.

"Just Myron and me."

"Perfect."

"We took two elevators up and up and up," I tell my parents later, "more than one hundred floors! I felt like a rocket. The top floor is called an observation deck. Manhattan really is an island. We could see the East River and the Hudson River. Mr. Lobos said the Bronx River is way north by Harlem, but we couldn't see it, too much air pollution. That's all the engine exhaust from the cars and trucks and buses--"

"--I felt like a rocket, too," Myron says. "It was fun."

"I want to go next time," Zenon whines.

We're having a late dinner. Mr. Lobos has ordered something for everyone called The Blue Plate Special. That's shreds of beef with vegetables and potatoes. The Blue Plate Special tastes better with ketchup all over it.

I eat all the way down to the plate. Who knew sightseeing could make someone so hungry? "The plate is blue," 'The blue plate special,' " I say in careful English.

Papa nods. "Your first full day in America, Pedrito, and you've already learned some English."

"Everyone is still asleep," I say as I open our hotel door in the morning.

Mr. Lobos shrugs. "Shall we go downstairs for breakfast?"

I dress quickly as my family sleeps on.

All day yesterday, the Buczkowskis moved as slowly as turtles. We wanted to stop and study the buses, the statues in Central Park, the flowers and trees, all the different cars and trucks, and the huge buildings called skyscrapers.

Mr. Lobos was always saying, "Let's keep moving."

We saw a car accident; one car rammed right into another one. Crash! No one on the sidewalk even stopped walking! The drivers jumped out of their cars and burst into shouting and arm waving.

"Someone will call for help," Mr. Lobos said. "Let's keep moving."

It's a curious feeling. Ever since we got off the plane, my parents have receded into the background. Mr. Lobos asks me where we'd like to go and what we'd like to do. Yesterday, he translated the information about the zoo animals into Spanish. After the first few exhibits Papa stopped asking me for the translations. Instead, he and just Mama tagged along behind us.

I mention this to Mr. Lobos at breakfast. "You feel like the adult, and your parents are like your children."

"That's right."

"Once you're home, your parents will become your parents again." Mr. Lobos stares into his coffee cup. "But outside the household ...as with my family, you and your brothers will assimilate much faster into American life than your parents ever will. They'll be strangers in a strange land."

"They were strangers in a strange land in Venezuela, too."

"Parents emigrate for their children, Pedrito. I'll be going to back to school in the fall. I'll continue my education." He taps his forehead. "Why are some people so timid, and others so bold? Why do some pick themselves up and thrive after trauma? Why do others falter and never recover? 'Trust in the Lord forever, for the Lord God is an everlasting rock.' Isaiah 26:4. Your parents aren't religious?"

"We've never talked about it. The nearest church was miles away. Mr. Lobos, where was God in Poland? I've always wanted an answer to that question."

He shakes his head sadly. "You've asked the wrong question, Pedrito. Where was man in Poland? We all know how we're supposed to treat one another. We all know."

At lunch, my stomach rumbles so loudly Mr. Lobos hears it. "The refugee's stomach. Americans eat so much meat. The rest of the world lives on rice and vegetables. You'll get used to it. What shall we do this afternoon? You leave tomorrow morning."

After I translate, Mama says in slow, careful English, "the Statue of Liberty, please."

Mr. Lobs sputters into his coffee with cream. He says in slow, careful English, “Okay, Mrs. Buczkowski, the Statue of Liberty.”

“What’s this, Papa?” I hold up a photograph of the New York City skyline, printed on thick paper. “It was on our desk in our hotel room.”

“That’s a postcard. I haven’t seen one since before the war. Write to Tolic to let him know we’ve arrived safely. I’ll give you our address in Cleveland. He can write back to you.”

“There’s a post office around the corner, but we should leave soon,” Mr. Lobos says. “The ferry won’t wait.”

We take a taxi to Castle Clinton on the south side of the island. Mr. Lobos buys our ferry tickets, compliments of the Mission. Once again, the Buczkowskis move like turtles—we want to take in the beautiful ferry with the polished wooden floors, and the other ships that line the harbor.

As we walk up the gangway, I hear Mama behind me muttering, “Paris,….France…Bonn, Germany…Ah…ah…Athens, Greece.”

“You sailed across the Atlantic Ocean on a ship, Mama,” I say in a hopeful tone, “when we first came to Venezuela.”

Mama's voice is shaking. "That was an ocean liner, Pedrito. This ferry is so small. These waves are so big."

Papa grasps her elbow.

On the ferry, Mama sits inside on a bench. She grabs onto a pole for dear life. The rest of us rush to the bow. When the ferry docks at Liberty Island, Papa helps Mama as she staggers down the gangway. The dark circles under her eyes are back.

Americans rush through the day so fearless and bold. They remind me of Dog. I know Mama has her problems, but it's only been in the last few days—since coming to America—that her problems have gotten bigger somehow. How are we going to live here, if Mama is so timid and scared?

Papa's eyes flash with impatience. "Courage, Katrina."

Lady Liberty is massive. We stand there open-mouthed, our heads up-turned as far as they'll go. The other passengers disembark and flow around us.

Zenon asks, "Is she holding a piece of fire?"

"In the sunlight, it looks like fire," Mr. Lobos says. "Her torch is covered in gold. Who's ready for some climbing?"

There's an iron gate in front of the stairway that goes up to her crown.

“What a disappointment.” Mr. Lobs points to a sign. “This says the crown is closed for repairs. Her crown is rarely safe. It’s usually closed. I was hoping it would be open.”

I translate. Mama says, “That’s all right. We’re here. We need to have a conversation, she and I. Excuse me.”

Mama walks all by herself to the end of Liberty Island. She turns and faces the statue. We watch, fascinated, as she talks and talks. She spreads her arms and lifts her head to shout although she’s too far away to hear anything.

Mr. Lobos arches his eyebrows at me. All I can do is shrug.

Papa says, “Tell Mr. Lobos that the very first conversation your mother and I ever had was about Lady Liberty. We were in the potato fields, in Hitler’s work camp in the dead of winter. She told me all her family had died just before Christmas, and as they died, none of them could understand why God had abandoned them. Your mother made a solemn promise to them all, that she would see the Statue of Liberty for their sakes, to be a witness to their deaths.

“The Nazis invaded Poland in 1939. It’s been almost twenty years. A promise kept.”

After I translate, Mr. Lobos says softly, “I was wrong about your mother, Pedrito. She’s one of the bravest women I’ve ever met. God abandons no one. Never, ever think that.”

Chapter Eighteen
Tío Frederick

Has it been only five days since Papa told us about the train and tunnels through the Allegheny Mountains of Pennsylvania?

As the train sways and rattles through the Pennsylvania countryside, I count on my fingers: today, we caught the train at 10:30 in the morning. Yesterday, the Statue of Liberty; three days ago, the Central Park Zoo and the Empire State building; four days ago, the long ride to the Caracas airport in the mayor's car, and the airplane to New York City; five days ago, our last breakfast in our house, our elegant lunch party at the Zimmer's, and Dog's new home.

It was just five days ago. It seems like weeks have passed, months, so much has happened in so little time. When I think about New Barcelona, I remember the slow, quiet days and the clear, sweet air.

Am I still Pedrito? Or am I becoming someone else? Am I an American boy—hurry, hurry, and hurry. Let's keep moving.

This morning, Mr. Lobos helped us buy the train tickets, with lunch and dinner included. He showed me the meal times on the tickets. "Pedrito, this means your family will be seated for lunch at 12:30, and dinner for 6:30."

I didn't remind him that we can't keep time. No wristwatches.

"Every third car has a bathroom." He jerked his head toward a shouting man. "He's calling your train. It's an Express. Don't get off the train until Cleveland! Someone will meet you there. You'll be fine."

Quickly, Mr. Lobos shook my father's hand, then mine. "Keep moving. You'll be fine." Another man in another uniform took us to our seats.

Mr. Lobos stood outside our window. He waved and waved as the train left Pennsylvania Station. When I could see him but he could no longer see us, Mr. Lobos glanced at his wristwatch and ran out of the station. Hurry, hurry, hurry.

We didn't have to worry about our lunch. Another shouting man in another uniform comes through the cars, announcing lunches served at 11:30, noon, and our time at 12:30. "Papa, how will we know when it's twelve-thirty?"

He points to the far end of the train car: a clock.

After lunch (something called hot dogs, potato chips, and applesauce) we returned to our seats. The gentle rocking of the train makes me so sleepy…

A braying voice shouts in English, "Six-thirty dinner seating, last call for the six-thirty dinner seating."

I wake with a start. Six-thirty. I understood what the braying man said! I am learning English! My family is fast asleep. Papa is snoring with his head against the seat back. Zenon is sleeping with his head in Mama's lap. Myron naps with his head on Mama's shoulder. Mama's tight, anxious face has smoothed into one of deep, deep sleep.

I shout, "Everyone has to wake up now. Dinner is right now."

Zenon stretches. "Did we miss the tunnels?"

Myron yawns. "Did we miss the chocolate?"

Dinner is cold chicken salad: delicious. And iced tea in a tall glass with a slice of lemon stuck on the rim. The waiter gives us spoons with long handles—the longest spoon handles I've ever seen. I hold it up to Mama and frown.

"That's an iced tea spoon. It's for stirring sugar into a tall glass. There was an elegant tea room in Warsaw before the war." Mama smiles at the memory. "Keep stirring or the sugar will drift to the bottom of the glass."

I stir my tea. "How will we know we're in Cleveland?"

Papa finds a stub of a pencil in his pocket and writes 'Cleveland' on his napkin. "When the train comes into a station, the name of the town or city will be on a sign above the platform. You boys look for the sign."

After dinner, we go back to our seats. I stay awake while everyone else falls asleep again. The outside lights flash across my family's faces the way heat lightening pulses in the jungle night sky back home.

It's 9:30 in New Barcelona. Everyone's asleep, including Dog. What must Dog be thinking? Does he miss me as much as I miss him?

Two hours later I see the sign: Cleveland.

"Papa! We're here. Hurry, hurry, hurry."

The Buczkowskis wake with a start. Papa and I pull our suitcases down from the racks. Mama grasps Myron's hand and Zenon's hand. We scramble down onto the platform....

…and no one holding a **Buczkowski** sign. Instead, there's a man who looks like my father. A man who looks like Papa? He has the same thin, blond hair looped from ear to ear around a balding head, the same bright blue eyes. That's impossible.

"Karol? I'm your cousin, Frederick. Thank God you're all alive."

"Frederick? At long last we meet."

Papa and his cousin embrace while Myron, Zenon, and I gape in astonishment. He's family, someone Hitler didn't kill in the work camps.

As Frederick shakes my hand I ask him, "How did you survive the work camp? Papa told me everyone in his family had died."

"We never saw the work camps. My family left Poland in 1935 and my father got a job at Republic Steel. Is it true, Karol? Everyone else is the family is gone? There's no one left in the old country?"

"It's true."

"Those Nazi pigs paid for it, serves them right. We pounded their cities to smithereens."

"What is 'smithereens'?" I ask.

"We knocked their cities flat. Flying Fortresses. B-17s. Air power. And East Germany is communist now. It serves them right.

"It's late and you must be tired. Let's go."

Frederick takes two of the suitcases and Papa takes the other one. We walk into a broad square. The Buczkowskis are turtles once again. We slooow down for a good look.

"This is Public Square," Frederick says. "You just left Union Terminal in Terminal Tower."

Mama says, "Look, a department store. Dresses, shoes, handbags."

Frederick says impatiently, "We've got a trolley to catch."

"Let's keep moving," I say in Spanish as my brothers laugh.

A trolley looks like a bus. Electricity crackles from a wire attached to the roof. The wire is attached to more wires hanging from the street poles. Myron leans far out the window to watch the crackles until Mama tells him to sit down.

Papa introduces us. Frederick asks my brothers and me to call him Uncle Frederick. "'Uncle', that's the English."

It's late, I'm tired, but inside I'm glowing. I have a *tío*, an uncle.

Fifteen minutes later we're walking down a narrow street.

"Here it is, home," Uncle Frederick says, "West Sixth Street, the Alley."

We gaze at a perfectly square brick building, perfectly dark.

"No electricity?" Papa asks.

"It has electricity. Everyone is asleep."

Uncle Frederick gives Papa the key. We walk up to the second floor and open the door to our new home. Three rooms—one large room with a kitchen and sitting room, a bedroom, and a bathroom. There's some furniture—chairs and a table in the kitchen, a sofa with a low table in front of it, a folded pile of blankets, pillows, and towels.

Zenon yawns.

"Time for bed," Mama says.

Uncle Frederick sleeps on the sofa. Myron, Zenon, and I sleep in blankets and pillows on the floor. For the first time since my parents got married, they have a bedroom of their own to sleep in.

I toss and turn for a long time. What did Uncle Frederick say about the Nazis? "We pounded their cities to smithereens."

By 'we' he didn't mean Poles. He meant Americans and the United States Army and Air Force. When did he start to think of himself as an American? Was it like the switch from awake to asleep? Or the opposite, from asleep to awake?

Definitely asleep to awake, for Americans are the most wide-awake people I've ever seen, always in a hurry, hurry, hurry. I wonder if I'll ever be in such a hurry. Even more, if I'll ever catch up.

Chapter Nineteen

Sé fuerte

The next morning, Uncle Frederick walks into the apartment with two paper bags full of food." There is a grocery store just around the corner."

We sit around our kitchen table as Uncle Frederick unpacks the bags. He opens the kitchen cabinets and cupboards and takes out dishes and cups, glasses, utensils, napkins and place mats.

Mama gasps. "Everything is new. Where did it all come from?"

Uncle Frederick smiles at Mama. "My wife bought it all, Katrina. You'll find pots and pans in the drawer under the stove and towels in the bathroom.

"Karol, I've found you a job. The Cleveland City Club needs a dishwasher and pot scrubber. The shift is one o'clock to nine o'clock. Can you start tomorrow? I'll go with you, and show you how to get there and back by trolley car. The club is downtown."

"Yes, thank you." Just like that, Papa has a job.

Uncle Frederick turns to Myron and me. "School starts on Wednesday. The Methodist Mission will pay for your shots and vaccinations. You'll go to my doctor. Your appointments are this afternoon. I'll pick you up in my car."

Myron whistles. "You have a car?"

Just like that, Myron and I have a school.

Papa takes a deep breath. "You have to understand, Frederick. We're used to the slow pace of village life, deep in the jungle. This past week has been so frantic. We've barely had the chance to catch our breaths."

"It's the routine you've lost, Karol. You'll settle into a different routine and you'll have time to catch your breaths again. You're all invited to my house this Sunday. My wife and children want to meet you."

Myron, Zenon, and I grin at one another. Just like that, we have cousins. American cousins.

My left arm throbs. Once Uncle Frederick explained to his doctor and nurses that Myron and I grew up in the South American jungle, a look of horror crossed their faces. First, they put masks over their noses and mouths, and then they must have given us every shot and vaccination they had. As we were leaving, the nurses sprayed something on all the waiting room armrests on the chairs and on all the door knobs.

"What were they spraying all over everything?" Myron wrinkles his nose. "It's soapy-smelling."

Uncle Frederick grins. "Bleach is a germ killer. South America has a lot of diseases that North America doesn't have. Let's get some ice cream. There's a Honey Hut ice cream parlor nearby. It's by the Zoo. We'll all have to go to the Cleveland Zoo sometime."

I wonder about Stefan. Is he recovering? If not, will his family take him back to the Yanomani village for more treatments? What would the nurses think of the Yanomani *chaman*? There's not enough bleach in the world.

I have a coconut ice cream bar covered in dark chocolate. Delicious.

Today is the first day of school.

Uncle Frederick is here, and watches us eat our eggs and rice. "I'll walk you both to school after you brush your teeth. Tomorrow, just follow the crowds of school kids. You can't miss them."

"Thank you, Frederick, what would we have done without you?" Mama smiles gratefully.

What would we have done without the Methodists and Mr. Lobos, too? We'd still be in in New Barcelona, with our friends, and Dog, and our comforting routine. Soccer every morning and Papa's onions and peppers for lunch….

Mama has been watching me. "You're nervous, Pedrito. I can see it in your face. Everything will be fine."

"We'll be late. We need to go," Uncle Frederick says.

Tremont Elementary School looks like our apartment building—a perfectly square, brick building but with three stories not two. But it's huge--the school takes up an entire block, with a playground behind it.

Uncle Frederick walks me to my classroom and tells me everything will be fine. He takes Myron by the hand and leads him down the hallway.

The New Barcelona playground rumor is true: my classroom is the same size of our entire school. There must be 50 classrooms in these long hallways, with students sorted by age.

Señoría Washburn shows me my seat. Everyone is staring.

I hear 'Pete Buczkowski' within the flood of English coming out of my teacher's mouth. She must have said something about books, because everyone is opening their desks and taking a big red book out of it. I open my desk. Like magic—the same book is inside.

The boy next to me has opened his book to the first page, first chapter. A stern portrait of Christopher Columbus glares out of the page. Next to Columbus is a drawing of Europe and North America, with a broad arrow pointing from Spain to Hispaniola.

Of course! *Norte Americanos* think it was Columbus who discovered America in 1492, for the king and queen of Spain. Everyone is South America knows it was the Chinese who discovered it first.

I raise my hand.

Señoría Washburn's eyebrows lift in surprise. "Pete?"

'Señoría, it is well known that North Americans believe it was the Spanish who first came to the Western Hemisphere. However, where I come from, Venezuela, we believe it was the Chinese who first came to the western shores of what is now Chile. Imagine if they'd stayed! We'd all be speaking… Chinese… instead…of Spanish." My voice winds down like a clock.

Everyone is staring, harder now. My teacher marches down the aisle. She says something, loudly. I must be giving her yet another baffled stare.

"Pete Buczkowski, English? Speak English?"

I understood her. Quickly, my mind runs through all the English words I know—Superman. Bang! Pow! Punch! Dog. President Rutherford B. Hayes. Lemonade Lucy. The Central Park Zoo. The Empire State building. The Statue of Liberty. Lunch 12:30. Dinner 6:30. Hamburgers. Ketchup. French Fries. The Blue Plate Special. Express. Hot Dogs. Potato Chips. Applesauce. Cleveland. Trolley.

My eyes burn with tears. What was I thinking? I don't speak English. So what am I doing here, in Cleveland, Ohio?

My teacher turns to a boy across the aisle from me. "Luis," she says before rattling off more English. Luis is shorter than me. He's the same soft brown color as Mr. Lobos's coffee and cream.

Luis pulls me to my feet, picks up my brand new notebooks and pencils, and walks me to the door. Once in the hallway, Luis looks left, right—there's no one in the hall.

"*Hola, amigo,* and here we may speak softly together in the language of our fathers, Spanish. No one is listening to us, Pete Buczkowski, although I'm guessing your friends call you Pedrito. Follow me."

Luis walks down one hallway and turns left down another. "You are from Venezuela? There they teach you the Chinese discovered America?" He shakes his head and laughs. “Don’t say that here, *amigo*. We may lose our Columbus Day holiday, a day off from school.”

“Luis, where are you from?”

“Puerto Rico. What is going to happen to you now happened to me exactly one year ago. *Sé fuerte!* Be strong! I’ll fetch you in one hour.”

Luis knocks on a door. Another teacher rolls her eyes as Luis rattles off something in English.

“Here you will sit, Pedrito, until you learn English. Learn as quickly as you can. Here are your notebooks and pencils. You will need them.”

The teacher points to a chair and desk much too small for me. Everyone stares once again, but these students are nowhere near my age. They look to be the same age as Myron, maybe eight years old.

The teacher is writing something on the blackboard:

See Alice run.

See Jerry run.

Alice and Jerry run after Jip.

Run, Jip, run!

A blond girl chatters next to me. She puts her book on my desk and points to a picture. A boy and a girl are chasing a dog and the dog has a ball in his mouth. 'Alicia' is a girl's name, in Spanish. 'Alice' must be the name in English. 'Jerry' must be the boy.

The words snap into place. The children are playing with this dog.

I copy the sentences into my notebook and create more sentences:

Jerry and Jip run after Alice.

Run, Alice, run!

Jip and Alice run after Jerry.

Run, Jerry, run!

The teacher smiles and puts a gold star on my paper.

"*Muchas gracias.*" I clamp my hands over my mouth. Thank you.

She gives me a wink. "*De nada.*" You're welcome.

An hour later, I have filled three pages with my own sentences in English. The teacher gave me a list of more Spanish-to-English verbs and prepositions.

Alice and Jerry eat the blue plate special.

Eat, Alice and Jerry, eat!

Jip and Jerry eat hamburgers and French fries.

Eat, Jip and the Jerry, eat!

Alice and Jerry see the lions and tigers.

See, Alice and Jerry, see!

Jerry and Jip run after the gorilla.

Run, gorilla, run!

The Buczkowskis fly from Venezuela.

Fly, Buczkowskis, fly!

The Buczkowskis see the Statue of Liberty.

See, Buczkowskis, see!

I'm trying to figure out how to write a sentence about my brothers and me turning an elevator into a rocket when Luis comes back. The teacher smiles at me and says something to Luis.

As we walk down the hall together, Luis explains. "Mrs. Kleinhammer says you're a fast learner, Pedrito. You should catch up soon. She'll give you homework for the weekend."

We sit down to math class. This I know. The numbers, the signs and co-signs, the co-efficients, add, subtract, multiply, divide, finish the equations, and show my work. This is an entirely different language, one I know very well.

Mrs. Washburn writes '100%' on my paper and gives me a long look.

The next class is science. I study the English words for the planets. Just like in Spanish, the planets are named for Greek and Roman gods and goddesses. All except the Earth. I wonder why?

A loud bell rings and I about jump out of my skin. Students run out of the classroom, and I run too.

Luis says, “Lunch time. See you at one-thirty.”

More students pour into the hallways. Myron won’t know the way back home. The thought of my brother wandering lost around Cleveland makes my heart pound. Where is he?

“Pedrito!”

Chattering students push a terrified Myron toward me.

“Myron, grasp my hand! Hold on, hard!” Students push against us like the Orinoco River at flood stage. In less than five minutes, the hallway is empty.

“Pedrito, what do we do?”

“We go home for lunch. I remember the way.”

Mama greets us at the apartment door. Zenon is twirling like a rocket with a big grin on his face.

The grocery store peppers aren’t as hot and delicious as Papa’s, the onions are too sweet, and the rice is mushy, but still, Myron and I eat as though we’re starving. We no longer drink guava juice. Instead, Mama pours milk.

She wants to know all about school. Myron starts talking about arithmetic and something called safe on the street. I let him talk on, only half listening until he starts talking about a brother and sister, and their dog.

"We had to copy a list of sentences about Alice and Jerry. They were running after their dog named Jip."

I drop my spoon. "I read about Alice and Jerry."

Myron shakes his head. "That can't be right. There's a boy from Cuba in my class. He said only the little kids read about Alice and Jerry. The big kids read about pioneers going into the American West."

My face burns as the horrible fact dawns on me. I'm learning English from the same reading book as Myron.

"Pedrito, what's wrong? More milk?"

"Nothing. We…we learned about the planets this morning. The English words for the planets are so similar to the Spanish ones."

If Papa were here, we'd talk about the Polish words for the planets, and the Polish astronomer Nicolas Copernicus.

But Papa is not here. His job takes him away from our lunch table, our dinner table. For the first two mornings, he joined us for breakfast but now he sleeps instead. He said washing dishes and scrubbing pans are much harder jobs than planting onions and peppers, but his hands have never been so clean.

We are all fast asleep by the time he comes home from work at the Cleveland City Club. We won't see Papa again until Saturday. His chair at our table is empty. It feels like a huge hole.

"Before you return," Mama says, "write notes to your father. He'll want to know what you've learned today."

"We have to be at school by one-thirty." Hurry, hurry, hurry.

"It won't take long, Pedrito. Your father wants to know about your lessons. There's nothing as important as a good education. Your father and I never had the chance."

Myron and I take pages out of our notebooks and sit down to write.

I write in Polish:

Papa,

Today we learned the names of the planets in English. They're similar to the names in Spanish. In both languages, the planets are named for Greek and Roman gods and goddess.

In arithmetic, we divided tens into hundreds and then hundreds into thousands. It was easy. We're going to learn the decimal system next.

I'm worried about the leaves. They're turning yellow, orange, and red. Is it because of the air pollution in America?

Myron wrote:

We learned about Alice and Jerry and their dog, Jip. We learned to subtract ones from tens. We learned about safe on the street.

"Very good," Mama says. "Uncle Frederick says you'll be home by three."

The next morning, a note from Papa is waiting for me on the table:

Pedrito,

Don't worry about the leaves. Northern leaves turn brilliant colors this time of year. I remember these vivid colors growing up in Poland. They fall to the ground and become fertilizer for the spring.

The Polish words for the planets are mostly from the Roman and Greek gods and goddesses, too. In Polish, the Earth is not named for a god or goddess. Is that also true in English and Spanish?

Did you know that the Polish astronomer Nicolas Copernicus is responsible for the heliocentric theory? In his day, people thought the

Earth was in the center of the Universe. Copernicus believed the sun was in the center of the Universe.

Now we know that isn't correct, either. The sun is in the center of our solar system. Copernicus's heliocentric theory changed the way people looked at the sky, and the world, and our place in it all.

I hope Cleveland is changing the way you look at the sky, the world, and our place in it all.

I'll see to you on Saturday, the day after tomorrow.

Papa

Sé fuerte, I think. Then I remember—Papa wouldn't know that phrase. He wouldn't know what I was talking about.

Myron and I walk to school by ourselves this morning.

Luis translates, as Mrs. Kleinhammer tells me take the Alice and Jerry reading book home with me. She says to read as much of the next chapter as I can, and do the homework after the chapter. She will grade it special, just for me, and answer any questions through Luis.

How can I do the homework and not let Myron know we're reading from the same book? I can't let Papa and Mama know it, either. I'm the older brother;

el hermano mayor, the one Myron and Zenon turn to for help and guidance.

I'll have to figure out a way to study in secret.

Chapter Twenty

The Green Light

I hide my Alice and Jerry book in my notebook and read it after Myron and Zenon are asleep. I write the homework in my notebook. I've been getting gold stars, but even the gold stars are embarrassing. Gold stars are for little kids, not for *el hermano mayor*.

Mama doesn't notice that's it's a book for babies. She sees the English and pats me on the head. "I'm proud of you for working so hard."

Papa won't be home for half an hour. I'll get as much of the homework done as I can before hiding the book again. Hurry, hurry, hurry.

On Sunday afternoon, Uncle Frederick picks us up in his car and takes us to his house. The American cousins we were looking forward to are twin girls just a little older than Zenon. Suzanne and Lisa chatter at us as they show off their dolls, their doll house, and a tiny, pink table with matching pink chairs.

Suzanne and Lisa put on floppy straw hats, sit at their table, and pretend to have tea from a miniature tea set. Zenon sits down with them, but I can't keep the disappointment from my face and neither can Myron. Six-year-old girls pretending to have a tea party! Our American cousins.

Myron and I join the adults in the back yard. The adults are sitting under a round table with an umbrella over it. Next to it is a long bench.

Uncle Frederick explains that his wife is Polish American, but doesn't speak Polish. My parents speak about as much English as they do Spanish. Every time my parents say something, Uncle Frederick has to translate. Every time Aunt Caroline says something, Uncle Frederick has to translate. He looks as frazzled as I felt, in New York City.

"Maybe you boys could help me out here?" Uncle Frederick asks.

"Of course," I say, but Aunt Caroline talks so fast, I can't translate for her and neither can Myron. She tries speaking louder but that doesn't help.

There are four good things about the afternoon. Uncle Frederick has something called a barbeque grill.

He cooked hamburgers and hot dogs, as many as we want. We eat something called potato salad and drink lemonade. Myron has two slices of chocolate cake with chocolate ice cream.

Another good thing is the bench. Just before we all sat down to eat Uncle Frederick pulled the bench backrest forward. It levered into a table, like magic. After we ate, Myron and I inspected the pulleys and levers.

"We're going to have some engineers in the family," Uncle Frederick said.

"Rocket scientists," Papa replied, "either the California Institute of Technology or the Massachusetts Institute of Technology. Cal Tec or MIT."

After our early dinner, Uncle Frederick brings out an American football. He teaches Myron and me how to throw it, "Keep your fingers up!" and how to catch it. It's fun.

"Learn to throw a football, boys. Every American boy knows how to throw and catch a football."

"It's like ketchup, then," Myron says.

Uncle Frederick scratches his head, but I know exactly what Myron means: football, ketchup, hamburgers, hot dogs, iced tea, chocolate cake, and lemonade. We are learning the American routine.

The fourth good thing is Uncle Frederick telling us that we don't have school tomorrow. It's an American holiday called Labor Day.

After three weeks of extra homework, I've finished the Alice and Jerry book. I know how to write English in the past tense and the future tense. I've tried to write a sentence about turning an elevator into a rocket, but it's just too complicated. There are too many things happening all at once—my brothers and me, the elevator, and the rocket. Somehow all these things link to coming to the United States of America to live. At that point, my sentence changes from things to thinking, to pretending, to wishing, to hoping, to Cal Tech and MIT. It's just too complicated.

Through Luis, Mrs. Kleinhammer tells me I'll start on the second Alice and Jerry book next week.

"A second Alice and Jerry book?" I ask in slow and careful English.

Mrs. Kleinhammer holds up three fingers. "There are three Alice and Jerry books, Pete."

I groan. Three books! I'll be hiding my homework for months. I'll be sitting with the little kids, and little kids are much harder to understand than adults. They talk too fast and their pronunciation is bad because of all their missing teeth. What a nightmare.

At lunch today, Myron talks about the playground. “There’s what looks like a hollow log. It’s called a slide. There’s leather straps attached to iron chains, and the chains are attached on top, those are called swings. And, a big wheel that the kids ride on, it’s called a Merry-go-Round. The playground is open after school. We could all go.”

“I want to go,” Zenon says.

Mama pours more milk. “That’s a wonderful idea. After school, the two of you will take Zenon to the playground.”

The playground, what a nightmare. Zenon wants me to push him way too high on the swings. The slide is way too steep for him. It’s not safe. He and Myron want to go way too fast on the Merry-go-Round. No matter how much I scold, they don’t listen.

Myron runs around and around a dirt ring called the bases on the playground’s softball field. He says he’s pretending to be Rocky Calivito, a baseball player for the Cleveland Indians.

“How do you know about him?”

“All the kids talk about him. Everyone runs around the bases and pretends to be Rocky Calivito.”

I want to ask him how he understands what all the kids say, but I don’t. Myron knows more English than I do? That can’t be. “It’s time to go home.”

"We just got here," Zenon whines. "I want the swings again."

"Myron and I have homework. When you're a student you'll have homework, too."

Myron narrows his eyes at me. "You sound like Papa."

Zenon whines again. "You sound like Mama."

"It's time to go home."

The next morning is a puppet show for Mrs. Kleinhammer's class. Would I like to attend? Sure, but I walk next to Mrs. Kleinhammer. Maybe people will assume I'm a teacher's helper or something.

I sit in the back of the gymnasium with the other teachers. The show is called Safe on the Street. We should look both ways before crossing the street. We should wait for the green light before crossing the street. Before and after school, we should wait for the crossing guard before crossing the street. We should walk at the crosswalk, and not between parked cars. Crossing between the parked cars is called Jay walking, of all things.

The puppets start to run across the street to chase balls, dogs and cats, friends, brothers and sisters, late for school, and ice cream trucks. They don't look both ways. They don't wait for the green light. They don't wait for the crossing guard. They cross between cars.

The children yell at the puppets. "Stop! Safe on the Street! Stop!"

I pay close attention because I don't do any of these things. There's a right way to cross an American street? I don't look both ways. How am I supposed to wait for a green light if I don't know where to find one? A crossing guard yelled at me once but I didn't understand her. I just kept walking, with Myron tagging after me.

I've crossed between parked cars—Jay walking is faster and easier than walking to the corner.

I've been crossing streets the wrong way all this time?

After the show, the teachers hold up different colored flags so the students will know what line to fall into.

I'm standing at the very end of Mrs. Kleinhammer's red-flag line when I hear in Polish, "What are you doing here?"

Myron is looking up at me, open-mouthed.

"I'm…I'm helping."

"Helping to do what? This puppet show is for second graders." Myron narrows his eyes at me. "What are you going here?"

"What's second grade?"

"I'm in second grade. What grade are you in?"

"I don't know. I'm in Mrs. Washburn's class."

I'm in a grade? I thought I was in a class.

Myron narrows his eyes again. "What are you doing here?"

"I'm...I'm going back to Mrs. Washburn's class. See you at lunch."

There's a little sign next to my teacher's door. Grade 6.

Grade six? I'm reading English four grades below where I'm supposed to be. No wonder Myron is suspicious. My face burns in shame.

It's after 9:30 and we're in math class. This is the best part of the day because math is a language I know backwards and forwards. Last week, Mrs. Washburn put me in a small group of students who understand as much math as I do; two boys and a girl, who all greeted me with big smiles.

We have our own math book, one with a big number 7 on it. I point to the 7. "Grade seven maths?" I ask the group in slow and careful English.

"That's right, Pete," the boy named Roger says. "We're a grade ahead of everyone else. Americans say 'math.' In British English it's 'maths.' "

"It's...what?"

"We have a rocket club," the girl named Cecilia says. "Do you like rockets?"

"I like rockets!"

"Great," Roger says. "Wednesday afternoons. You have to know a lot of math to launch rockets. We're The Tremont Rocket Club."

"Please, what is 'launch'?"

The group gapes at me. The boy named Dennis puts his hands together. "Swoosh!" he says as he lifts his hands toward the ceiling.

"You launch rockets?" I'm dumbfounded.

The Tremont Rocket Club looks at Dennis. "Well," he says, "we're trying to launch them."

Mrs. Washburn frowns in our direction. "Shhh."

On the way home for lunch, I watch Myron. He looks both ways, up and down the street. What's he looking for? At our corner, he stops, looks up, and stares toward the center of the street. There's a red light hanging from the center. In a minute, maybe less, the red light turns off and a green one turns on. Myron crosses the street toward home.

"What are you looking for? Why did you wait for that green light? Aren't you hungry?"

"The cars might hit us. 'Safe on the Street'."

"But the cars always stop for us. Aren't they supposed to stop?"

"No, Pedrito. We're supposed to stop for the cars. 'Safe on the Street'."

"Where did you learn this?"

"In second grade," Myron says in an exasperated voice. "That puppet show this morning was a treat for everyone who scored well on the 'Safe on the Street' test."

"We didn't have that test. I'm in the sixth grade."

"What were you doing with the second graders, then?"

I punch Myron's arm, much harder than I meant to punch him.

"Ow, you'll pay for that."

At lunch, Zenon chatters away about rockets. Myron glares at me while we eat our peppers, onions, and rice.

"That reminds me, Mama. I was invited to join a rocket club today."

"I want to be in the rocket club," Myron says.

"It's only for six graders, not second graders."

"Mama, Pedrito punched me." Myron shows off his bruised left arm before he runs into the sitting room.

"Pedrito, why would you do such a thing?" Mama's eyes fill with tears. "This family has suffered enough violence, why?"

"I knew it, I knew it, I knew it!" Myron shouts as he holds my Alice and Jerry book above his head.

"Where did you get that?" I lunge at the book.

"I found it in your notebook. You think you know so much English, Pedrito, but you don't know any more English than I do. You don't know how to cross a street, either."

"Give me that!" I chase Myron around the kitchen table.

"Stop it, Stop it!" Mama stands in front of Myron and grabs my book from his hand.

"What is happening to this family?" Mama asks. "The two of you, sit down." Mama takes a whimpering Zenon into her lap. "Pedrito, is this your book?"

"I'm in the sixth grade. I'm in the seventh grade math group, that's a year ahead of everyone else. I was invited to join The Tremont Rocket Club."

"Is this your book?"

"Yes," I whisper.

"I knew it, I knew it, I knew it," Myron crows. "You don't know any more English than I do." Myron points to the book. "That's a second grade reading book, Mama."

"Myron, we all came to America on the same day. Didn't we?"

Myron's mouth drops open.

"The two of you, write to your father. His responses will be waiting for you tomorrow at breakfast."

Myron looks at me in triumph. "I knew it."

"That's enough, Myron. Families stick together. You should be grateful you have an older brother. Both of mine are dead. Older brothers look out for younger brothers."

Myron hangs his head. "Yes, Mama."

Papa,

You don't understand this Spanish term: I am *el hermano mayor*. The older brother is supposed to help the little brothers—*los hermanitos*. Myron acts like he doesn't need my help but he does.

We're learning the decimal system. Did you know the decimal system was invented by Frenchmen after their Revolution?

I steal a glance at Myron's letter. **Not fair Not Fair NOT FAIR** he's screaming in Polish in inch-tall letters. **NO ENGLISH** he screams in two-inch tall Polish letters.

The next day at breakfast, our letters are waiting for us, propped up against two coffee cups. Myron snatches his up, reads it quickly, scowls, and stuffs the letter in his pocket.

Maybe mine is better? It's a longer letter. Papa's neat, Polish script fills two-thirds of a page.

Pedrito

I know what *el hermano mayor* means. I didn't learn Spanish in school, but I did live in a Spanish speaking country for more than ten years. I picked up words and phrases here and there. Here in Cleveland, I read the newspaper every day to learn English.

Yes, you are the older brother to Zenon and Myron, but I am their father. This should be a relief to you. I'm sorry I see the three of you only on weekends now, but your brothers answer to me, and not to you. Again, this should be a relief.

As to English, the important thing is you're working hard to learn it. This is the country where you can do anything you want, there are no barriers, but you have to speak and read English in order to do what you dream of doing.

Your mother tells me you were invited to join a rocket club, and you are in seventh grade math. Very, very good.

I'll see you on Saturday, that's just six days from now.

Papa

Six days! An eternity. Myron and Zenon may answer to you, Papa, but I have to keep my eye on them. That's not a relief.

Chapter Twenty-One
Dog Redux

At Wednesday lunch, Zenon asks, "Pedrito, can we go to the playground after school today?"

"No. Wednesday afternoon is The Tremont Rocket Club. After school, we walk across the street to the junior high school and a science teacher named Mr. Ripley helps us. He's our sponsor."

Last week, Mr. Ripley talked about propulsion thrust. There's a formula for enough fuel to create enough thrust to launch a rocket out of our atmosphere. After he wrote the formula for propulsion thrust on the blackboard, I was astounded that I understood him.

I wanted to explain what the thrust felt like when our airplane left the Caracas airport, but I just couldn't pull the words together.

Just as Papa said in New York City, I understand the spoken language the more I hear it. The words just snap into place. Papa brings the newspaper home from work and I can read bits and pieces of the articles. I read part of an article in the sport section about Rocky Calivito to Myron and pointed to his photograph in his Cleveland Indians uniform. Myron was impressed.

Reading is the fastest way for me to understand English. It's the speaking that's hard.

Zenon kicks me under the table. "Playground."

"Stop kicking, Zenon. Myron will take you."

Mama shakes her head. "Myron is much too young to take Zenon to the playground. Pedrito, you'll have to give up your rocket club."

I look at Mama in alarm. "I can't do that."

"Family comes first—"

"--Mama, you could take us to the playground," Myron says.

"Impossible." Mama waves her spoon in the air. "I don't know where it is."

"I know where it is. Pedrito and I have been walking to school for nine weeks. I can teach you 'Safe on the Street.' "

"Impossible."

I put my spoon on my plate. “Mama, when was the last time you were out of this apartment?”

“I…I don’t like Cleveland. The sidewalks feel bumpy against my feet. There’re too many trees. It reminds me of the jungle. The two of you can take Zenon to the playground.”

I say, “Cleveland isn’t anything like the jungle.”

Myron puts his spoon on his plate. “You wouldn’t set foot in the jungle, either. Why are you afraid of everything? Afraid is boring.”

“When was the last time Zenon was out of this apartment?” I ask.

Mama’s voice is shaking. “He needs to go to the playground with you and Myron. That’s why you’ll have to give up rocket club.”

“I’ve been invited to join the checkers club,” Myron speaks up, “on Monday afternoons. I’m going. There’s Little League baseball in the spring. I can run the bases as fast as Rocky Calivito. I’m going.”

“Dennis from The Tremont Rocket Club has invited me to his house on Friday afternoons to watch *The Adventures of Superman.* I’m going.”

“I want to go, too,” Myron says.

“I want to go to the playground!” Zenon wails.

"What is happening to this family?" Mama asks faintly. "We've scattered in a hundred different directions."

"Mama, does Papa know you haven't left the apartment since Uncle Frederick's barbeque?"

"Pedrito, you're being disrespectful--"

"You've been lying to Papa," Myron interrupts. "You've been telling him that YOU"VE been taking Zenon to the playground. You've BEEN LYING."

"PLAYGROUND!" Zenon shrieks. "PLAYGROUND!"

"I don't have to listen to this." Mama jumps from the table, runs into her bedroom and slams the door.

Silence. Even Zenon has stopped shrieking.

My brothers and I look at one another. The only sound is the cars, driving back and forth on West 6th Street.

"*Mi hermano mayor*, what do we do?" Myron asks.

"I don't know."

Myron snaps his fingers. "We'll write Papa a letter."

"She'll tear it up."

"We'll write it in Spanish."

"Papa doesn't read Spanish."

"English, then."

"Papa doesn't read English, either."

Myron stares at me in shock. "We can't do anything until Saturday? That's three days from now."

I slam my fist on the table. "Those Nazi pigs! Those *Niemskie swinie!* They were supposed to stay behind. But they're here. The Nazis followed us to here to Cleveland."

"If the Nazis followed us here to Cleveland, can they take me to the playground?"

"No, Zenon, no." I put my head in my hands.

Myron picks up his spoon. "Look, everything's going to be fine, but you can't go to the playground today."

I say slowly, "Everyone's always saying that: in Polish; in Spanish; in English. But nothing's fine." I shout toward the bedroom door. "Nothing's fine."

A soft, whispery sound from the other side of the bedroom door; Mama has pulled the blankets over her head.

"That would be funny though, wouldn't it?" Myron chuckles. "Hitler pushes Zenon on a swing. Hitler helps Zenon up the slide ladder. Hitler pushes the Merry-go-Round."

"I'd laugh at that."

"Tell Hitler I like to swing high. I need big pushes. Big."

"Big pushes, Zenon. Sure. Everything's fine."

Zenon opens the bedroom door and runs inside. "Mama! Hitler will take me to the playground."

Mama moans.

"Pedrito," Myron says softly. "What if Mama had problems in her head before the Nazis? Remember what Papa said at the Statue of Liberty? It's been almost twenty years since the Nazis invaded Poland."

"I—I—never--thought of that," I stammer. We've always blamed Mama's terrors on the Nazis. Always. Papa's kitchen chair is empty, and now Mama's kitchen chair is empty, too. A huge hole just got two times bigger.

Papa is home for weekends, so Saturday Food Feast is a different kind of celebration now. We don't play our 'in what country' game anymore, because we're here. We're here in the United States of America. My family thought all our problems would go away once we got our visas. I know Papa thought so. I see how tired he is and the sadness in his eyes. Cleveland is nothing like he thought it was going to be.

We have new problems mixed with the old. Last Sunday, two Methodists came over with winter coats.

Papa thanked them, and while Mama was in the kitchen cooking lunch, he stuffed the coats under the sofa. The Methodists looked at him strangely. Papa asked Myron and me to thank them while he held the door open.

The woman scolded me. "You'll need those coats, young man. Cleveland winters are brutal."

"Brutal?"

"Hard," the man said. "Very cold. Snow."

"Need coats. Yes. Snow. Yes. Thank you, thank you. Good-bye."

"When will we wear our winter coats, Papa?" Myron asked.

"I don't know. Maybe never," Papa had replied cheerfully as he shut the door. "Let's keep warm thoughts."

"Who was that?" Mama asked as she brought our lunch to the table. "No one important, Katrina." Papa gave my brothers and me a hard stare. Of course--he didn't want Mama to be reminded of the cold.

"You're quiet tonight, Pedrito. This is Food Feast night."

Papa's words brought me into the present with a start.

"Remember our 'in what country' game? I was just thinking, there was a rumor in New Barcelona. A typical American school is bigger than our entire village. It's true. Tremont Elementary is bigger than our village. The junior high across the street is even bigger."

"Look outside!" Myron shouts.

As fast as flying birds, a brisk wind is blowing snowflakes against our sitting room windows.

"The 'Witch of November,' " Papa says in dread, and in English, before switching back to Polish. "Some people at work said we were supposed to get a sudden drop in temperature and a snowstorm from Canada. Sometimes it happens in mid-November."

Myron and Zenon dive under the sofa for the winter coats. Myron pulls something that look like socks out of his pockets. "What's this, Papa? Socks?"

"Those are socks for your hands. Mittens."

"I have socks for my hands, too." Zenon holds up his mittens.

My winter coat has spider-y shaped socks in the pockets. "More socks?"

"Gloves. Take your brothers outside. It's your first snowstorm."

The big snowflakes are as light as feathers, but they sting like ice. We copy the neighbor kids—the Kramers—and hold our tongues out to catch snow. A snowflake feels like the shave ice Señor Nicholas used to buy us after Saturday market day, but it has no taste.

Snow blows against my face. It feels like the long-ago ice chip Mama put on my cheek when I was five, at the mayor's Christmas party.

We copy the Kramers again as Stuart and Bobbie take big steps, kicking the snow out in front of us. Snow creeps between my ankles and my pant legs. It cuts like a knife on my bare skin.

It's snowing so hard I can't see ten feet in front of me.

Stuart Kramer calls out, "It's a whiteout, Pete. Hope for more whiteouts—heavy snow means no school the next day."

The opposite side of the street has vanished in the heavy snow fall. Like magic, a whiteout is like magic.

"Look at the streetlamps," Myron yells.

The streetlamps shine down in cones of soft yellow, with snow blowing sideways across them. Snow falls on cars and nestles into the bare branches of the trees. It falls onto West 6th Street, turning it from shiny black to fluffy white. A car drives by slowly and its tires melt the snow into two black tracks.

Snow absorbs sound. We yell and our voices are as muffled as whispers. Cars drive past us quiet as jaguars stalking their dinners though the jungle. The wind murmurs softly through the bare trees. Even the constant pounding of the steel mills is as muted as a baby's breath as he sleeps.

All I can see is snowflakes, the soft yellow light from the streetlamps, and a purple, twilight sky. Magic.

Papa comes outside in a long winter coat. The four of us make a snowman, about as big as a chicken. Papa promises a bigger snowman later in the winter when there's more snow.

There's going to be more snow?

He shows us how to throw snowballs, and the Buczkowskis and the Kramers have a snowball fight, with parked cars as our fortresses.

"A flying fortress," I yell as I hurl a snowball over a Buick.

"B-17s," Stuart Kramer yells back as he pitches a snowball over an Oldsmoble.

Soon my ears and cheeks are burning: Fire and ice, always different and always the same.

"We need to come inside," Papa says. "You boys aren't used to the cold. I'll ask the Methodists for boots and snow hats."

"Next time, Buczkowskis," Stuart yells.

"The Witch of November," Myron yells back. Stuart's *hermanito,* Bobby, tosses a snowball right in Myron's face.

"Next time, Kramers." I throw a snowball at Stuart, who doesn't duck in time. Snow splatters all over the front of his coat. "Smithereens," I yell. Laughing, we four run into the apartment trailing snow and glory.

"We played in snow, Mama," Zenon shouts. "Where's Mama?"

We look in every closet, every corner.

"Found her," Myron says.

Mama's hiding in the far corner of her bedroom. Her knees are drawn up to her chin. She's trembling. Her face is as white as the snow.

"Oh, no, oh no," Papa says again and again.

"So cold, so cold," Mama says again and again.

They could be singing a duet.

Mama spends a long, long Sunday in bed.

Papa cooks for us. "The Blue Plate Special," he says cheerfully. We eat but his hot dogs and peppers are burnt. The hot dogs are wrapped in bread, not resting in hot dog buns.

I look forward to tomorrow, when I can be at school again.

"Will you cook us our lunch, tomorrow?" Myron whispers at the kitchen table. It's the evening and we're doing our homework. Mama is in her bedroom, Papa is on the sofa trying to read a week's worth of newspapers.

"What's going to happen to Zenon?" I whisper back. "It'll be like he's all alone. He can't be all alone."

Mama's voice echoes in my mind, *"You'll have to give up rocket club."*

Will I have to give up school, too? Someone has to take care of Zenon. "I just started school. I can't give up school."

Myron shrugs. "The snow's melted. Maybe Mama will get out of bed."

Tonight I toss and turn in my bed made of blankets and pillows. The sitting room floor never felt this hard and uncomfortable.

Behind their bedroom door, Mama and Papa are talking long into the night. Mama weeps. I hear short, barking sounds and with a shock I realize that's Papa sobbing. I've never heard him cry before, never.

"We're in trouble, we're in trouble," I say to myself again and again. America is nothing like we thought it would be.

Just before dawn, Mama woke us all up with a nightmare, the first she's had since coming to America. Whimpering Zenon crawls into my lap for comfort, but this time Myron sits on the sofa and scowls.

"This is ridiculous," he keeps saying with his arms across his chest.

Mama did make us breakfast, and lunch, but she won't talk. Zenon pesters about Hitler—when will he come by, and take him to the playground?

"Not today, Zenon. Everything's going to be fine."

A letter is waiting for me after school. Tolic's clear and precise Spanish handwriting marches across the thin Venezuelan Airmail pages.

***Hola*, Pedrito,**

I have the best news. After waiting for years and years, the Commonwealth of Australia has given my family visas! We are moving to Australia as quickly as possible. The Australians are going to help my father build a new eyeglass factory in the city of Melbourne. You must remember, he owned an eyeglass factory in Berlin before he and Mama fled to Venezuela.

Papa always said no good would ever come from Adolf Hitler and his brown-shirted, Nazi thugs. He was right, except—we're moving to Australia! I'll see kangaroos and koalas, cassowaries and kookaburras! Maybe a duck-billed platypus!

I'm sure you're wondering—what will happen to Dog?

"What will happen to Dog?" I say—my heart in my throat.

Zenon looks up from the toy cars the Methodists gave him. Myron stayed after school for his checkers club. Papa is working. Mama is lying in bed with the blankets pulled over her head.

"So cold, so cold," she moans again and again.

Don't worry. Papa bribed a lot of people so we could put Dog on a Pan-American flight to the Cleveland airport. He bribed more people to bring Dog to your house on West 6th Street, the Alley. Yes, I did get your postcard from NYC. You are so lucky to have seen the sights.

You'll have lots of room in your backyard chicken coop. By now, you must have a lot of chickens so Dog will feel right at home.

Papa thinks Dog will be at your house by Monday, November 17th.

Papa thinks it might be cold in Cleveland this time of year. Is that true? Have you seen any snow? Where will you keep Dog if there's snow?

Mama wrote to Her Royal Majesty's Orchid Society of Melbourne, and they wrote back...

"Zenon—today is Monday, November 17th."

"Grrummmm..." Zenon is pushing his cars around on the rug.

"Dog is coming here today."

Zenon jumps up from the floor. "Dog! Dog!" he yells just as someone pounds on our door.

At the door is a man in a uniform. "Is this your rooster? He sure talks funny. He's hungry. He keeps trying to bite my fingers."

"This is my rooster," I say in slow and careful English.

"*Mi hermanito,*" Zenon runs out in the hallway.

A big crate is covered with the United States Department of Fish and Wildlife, the United States Department of Natural Resources, the United States Department of Customs and Immigration, the United States Department of Agriculture, the United States Postal Service, and the United States Department of Land Management stickers all over the crate's wiring.

Dog looks right at me through an open patch. His chicken eyes bug out in surprise.

"Dog? I can't believe it."

Bwarf. Bwarf.

Chapter Twenty-two

The Pursuit

"You need to sign this form, boy. And this one. And this one."

The man in the uniform holds out papers, which I sign, and sign, and sign. Zenon is running up and down the hallway. Myron comes home from his checkers club.

"Dog is here!" Zenon shouts. Myron runs up and down the hallway with Zenon.

"Dog!" they yell in unison as they flap their arms like chicken wings.

Finally, I've signed all the forms. The man in the uniform helps me shove the crate through our apartment door. Zenon and Myron rush inside.

"Is there an adult here?' the man asks. "Are you kids all by yourself?"

"Our mother has sleep…is sleeping,"

"Then she can sleep through anything." The man shrugs and closes the door behind him.

Bwarf. Bwarf.

It's Dog, a jungle araucana, a South American *gallo*, in snowy and freezing Cleveland, Ohio.

"Let Dog out," Zenon says. "Maybe he'll catch a giant spider."

"Or he'll trick another *serpiente de cascabel.*" Myron peers into the crate.

I use a kitchen knife to pull the crate door open. In a flurry of bwarfs and feathers, Dog bursts out. He lands on the sofa. He flaps to the kitchen and lands on the kitchen table, where Papa has a week's worth of *Cleveland Plain Dealer* newspapers. Dog knocks them over. They flutter to the floor like chickens diving after dried corn in a coop.

Bwarf. Bwarf.

Tolic said we could put Dog in our backyard chicken coop. We don't have a chicken coop. We don't even have a backyard. How can a thirty-five pound rooster live in a second floor, one-bedroom apartment with a staircase?

Dog tears off a long strip of newspaper and eats it, just like he used to do back in New Barcelona. Myron fills a bowl with water. Dog drinks four times.

Our rooster flaps to the newspapers and shreds the sports section and the classifieds into a soft nest. He folds his legs under him and fluffs out his feathers. He blinks, slower and slower. Soon Dog is tucking his beak under his right wing. In no time at all he's fast asleep.

I say, "The trip must have worn him out."

"How on earth is Dog sleeping under our kitchen table?" Mama is standing in the kitchen's threshold, in a nightgown and sweater.

I show Mama Tolic's letter. "Pedrito, you know I can't read this."

"Tolic and his parents are moving to Australia so he sent us Dog."

Mama stares wide-eyed at sleeping Dog while we all wait in silence. What will she do with Dog? It snowed again last night. He can't live outside, wouldn't the cold kill him? What do Ohio farmers do with their chickens in the winter? Maybe there aren't any farmers in Ohio.

Could Dog live here, with us?

"Can you imagine it?" Mama shakes her head. "Dog came all the way from New Barcelona to Cleveland."

"We did too," Myron says.

"Ah, but we knew we were coming here. We traveled as a family. We knew the Methodists were expecting us. Someone put Dog in a crate and put the crate on a truck to Caracas. Someone else put Dog in the belly of an airplane and flew him to Cleveland. Someone else brought him here. Dog had no idea where he was going or what would happen once he arrived.

"Look at him. Instead of running around like a chicken with his head cut off, he's asleep. That takes courage."

"He knows he's safe, Mama."

"Yes, he does, Pedrito. He knows he's safe with his family and home again. He must be hungry."

Zenon says, "Dog ate some newspaper. He drank some water."

"That's no dinner. I'll make him something special."

My brothers and I stare at Mama as she opens cupboards, pours ingredients into bowls. We couldn't shake her out of her terrors, but Dog could. She hums as she stirs, then lights the stove.

"Why don't you boys go outside and play in the snow for a while? Dinner will be ready in about thirty minutes."

Just yesterday, Methodists stopped by with knitted hats and boots. We dress for winter and go outside. The Kramers are already on the sidewalk. We have another snowball fight, with parked cars as our fortresses.

For dinner, Mama made *cachapas,* her pancakes made from fresh corn, for the first time since coming to the United States. This is Dog's favorite meal. The corn kernels came out of the can but no one complained, especially Dog.

He sits between Zenon and me, just like he did back in New Barcelona. Dog remembers that good things to eat come from Zenon's plate. But this time we all took turns feeding him and he ate every bite.

We ate *cachapas* and rice, with tomatoes out of a can. Delicious.

"Dog can't use our inside toilet, Mama. What will he do when he has to check the horses' blankets?"

"Your father brings home the newspaper, Zenon. We'll train Dog to use the newspaper. I'll ask your father to bring home more. That will have to do. Dog has come all this way by himself. He gives everyone courage, doesn't he?"

"Sure, Mama." I agree.

"Don't let him tear up another sports section," Myron says.

That night, Papa wakes me up. “Pedrito, we have to talk.”

I’m rubbing my eyes as I sit up and look at the clock. It’s past eleven. I haven’t been awake this late since Uncle Frederick greeted us at the Cleveland train station.

“Anatole Zimmer sent Dog here? That’s what your mother said.”

I have Tolic’s letter tucked under my pillow. I show it to Papa.

“I can’t read this.”

“He likes to be called Tolic, Papa. Not Anatole. His family is moving to Australia so he sent Dog to Cleveland.”

“Dog can’t stay here.”

Now I’m wide awake. “Where’s Dog?”

“He’s made a nest for himself under the kitchen table.”

“Mama said to bring home more newspapers.”

Papa sighs. “I bring those newspapers home to read, as a way to learn English. I don’t bring them home for Dog.”

“Mama said Dog can live with us.” Awake. Switch. Asleep. I fall into my nest of blankets and pillows and tumble back into sleep.

It's become a routine, of sorts. Myron, Zenon, and I feed Dog some of our breakfast every morning before school. Dog likes bread crusts. At lunch, we're careful not to feed him bits of hot dog. Dog likes our lunches of rice, peppers, onions, and tomatoes better, so Mama makes a Venezuelan lunch, instead of an American lunch.

She's left a trail of newspapers all around the apartment for Dog, and he's pretty good about using them instead of the carpet.

Papa keeps shaking his head. "We're not allowed to keep pets in this apartment. What if we have to leave? It's called eviction. Where will we go?"

Meanwhile, like a launched rocket, my English is accelerating faster, faster, faster. Reading is the fastest, then listening, but my speaking just plods along. I will never assume that someone who doesn't speak a language well doesn't understand it. Speaking English is hard because all the words I could be using jumble together and then I forget how to do the tenses.

No one in Mrs. Washburn's class has ever heard of President Rutherford B. Hayes, even though he's from Ohio. When I tell them he's the most famous and beloved of all American presidents in South America, they look puzzled.

Rebecca Lichtenstein asked me why, but I couldn't explain about the Paraguayan vs. Uruguayan war, about a stretch of land called the Chaco, and how much he helped both nations when the war was over.

"President Hayes is beloved," I said. "I can't explain."

Mrs. Washburn has portraits and famous sayings from other presidents on her walls. Abraham Lincoln, Thomas Jefferson, Theodore and Franklin Roosevelt, and Harry Truman and more are all represented.

Theodore Roosevelt said, "Walk softly and carry a big stick." That I understand. Franklin Roosevelt said, "A day that shall live in infamy." I don't know what 'infamy' means.

Truman said, 'The buck stops here.' Abraham Lincoln said, " 'Four score and seven years ago, our fathers…' and Thomas Jefferson said …'the pursuit of happiness.' " I know these words are English, but they make no sense.

Just before the Thanksgiving holiday, I have enough English to ask. "Mrs. Washburn, What does 'four score' mean?"

"A 'score' is the old-fashioned word for twenty years. So, four score and seven years ago means eighty-seven years ago. President Lincoln gave this speech in

November 1863. Pete, what had happened eighty-seven years before?"

"I don't know."

She writes on the board:

1863

-87

1776

"This president," she points to Thomas Jefferson, "wrote the Declaration of Independence in 1776." I must be giving her a baffled stare. "The American Revolution started."

"Ah! Independence Day. *Los fuegos artificiales.*"

Mrs. Washburn frowns. "Fireworks?"

"Yes."

"'Score' was an old-fashioned word when Lincoln was alive, so he was giving us the sense of reverence for the past, a respect for a bygone time and for our ancestors. Lincoln was a great president and he was also a great writer. He had a way with words."

"Ancestors?"

"That's family who lived before us."

"Thomas Jefferson wrote, 'The pursuit of happiness.' What does 'pursuit' mean?"

"Chasing or hunting."

“Not catching? Not enjoying?”

“No, not catching. Jefferson never said we’re entitled to happiness. He never said there’s a guarantee. He said we should have the freedom to chase it. Jefferson said our freedoms have been given to us by God.”

“‘The buck stops here?’” I put my open hands on my temples to suggest antlers.

“What? No, no. A ‘buck’ is another word for a dollar. It means…ah, this is a hard one. It means…the president takes responsibility. He doesn’t make excuses when things go wrong.”

“So…God gave Americans the freedom to pursue happiness.”

“Not just Americans, Pete. Everyone.”

“Everyone?” I shake my head. My parents under the Nazis had no freedom and certainly no happiness. At the Statue of Liberty, Mr. Lobos told me God abandons no one. Freedom, tyranny, God, and chasing happiness: the United States has given me a lot to think about.

We have Thanksgiving dinner at Uncle Frederick’s. At dinner, Aunt Caroline explains about the traditional food. For Thanksgiving, Americans eat roasted turkey, dressing, (which is bread in crumbles and then baked again), gravy, (which is a turkey-flavored sauce), a purplish-red fruit called cranberries, corn, beans, and a pie made from a pumpkin, *la torta de calabaza.*

Uncle Frederick takes a deep breath to start to translate but I stop him.

"I understand what Aunt Carolina said, Uncle Frederick. I can translate for my parents."

In Polish, I speak about the Pilgrims and the food they ate at the first Thanksgiving in Plymouth. Cranberries are from Massachusetts, and wild turkeys are a North American bird. Myron doesn't know the story, so he listens, too. Only Zenon and the twins keep eating.

"So, a day to celebrate the harvest," Papa says.

"That's right; to celebrate the blessings God has given us."

"Good job, Pete," Uncle Frederick says. Aunt Caroline says I may have an extra slice of pie. A pie made from a pumpkin is delicious.

We come home late. Dog is fast asleep under the kitchen table, in a huge nest. He's shredded all the newspapers Papa brought home.

The apartment reeks; it smells like our chicken coop did, back in New Barcelona. It's much too cold to open the windows.

I'd forgotten how much time Dog used to spend outdoors. He'd run down the jungle trails with his quarry or he'd run down the trails just for the fun of it. We'd see his golden tail feathers bobbing above the broad leaves. Dog liked to run down the sidelines as we played in our soccer field. He used to follow me everywhere, unless Zenon or Myron distracted him somehow. He was always at my heels.

Zenon pesters relentlessly to go outside to the playground or to play in the snow. If Zenon isn't happy indoors all the time, how does Dog feel about it? He's half wild and the jungle is calling, even if that jungle is winter in Cleveland.

Papa sighs as his shoulders cave in. "My newspapers. I was going to read them tomorrow on my day off from work. I was looking forward to it, my chance to learn some English."

"Mama said Dog could stay. Where will he go?" I ask, as Myron and Zenon look at Papa anxiously.

"We can put his crate outside in the Alley."

"It's so cold, Karol," Mama says softly. "Dog is so good for our family. He'll die in the cold."

Papa sighs again. "I know it's late but we need a family meeting. Everyone sit down around the table."

Dog wakes up. Zenon feeds him a leftover *cachapas,* cold from the refrigerator.

Dog sits quietly under my feet. Does he know how much trouble he's in? Papa's trying to learn English, too. Dog can't shred all his newspapers.

"Pedrito, I'll ask for a lot more newspapers from the members of The Cleveland City Club. But I can't explain why—I don't have the English. You're going to make a sign for me to bring to work. Ask for extra newspapers for me to bring home. Americans always want to know why. State why. Tell them about Dog and what a rare rooster he is. Your teacher will help."

"I remember how you used to read newspapers in New Barcelona," I say, "but they don't help much, do they, to learn a language, I mean?"

"Immigrants study English at night, but I work at night. Newspapers are my only chance," Papa says sadly.

"There must be morning English classes." Myron gives me a sly grin. "There's Mrs. Kleinhammer's English class."

"I finished the third Alice and Jerry lesson last Friday. I'm done with second grade English."

"Oh, Pedrito," Papa says with tears in his eyes. "I'm so proud of you."

Chapter Twenty-three

How to Turn an Elevator into a Rocket

What did Papa used to say about the cold? Imagine the loneliest and saddest I have ever felt, plus exhausted, hungry, forsaken, and hopeless.

I don't feel that way about the cold. Snow looks peaceful as it falls outside our sitting room windows. I have sweet dreams, when I'm all wrapped up in my blankets and pillows and watching the snow fly before I go to sleep. Snow means snowball fights with Stuart and Bobby Kramer. Stuart keeps saying a blizzard means a snow day—that means no school the next day.

It's Monday, the first day of December, and the wind blows cold. Snow is blowing against our faces as Myron and I run to school. Students throw snowballs at the snow trucks because they're plowing the streets, scraping them down to the bare pavement. The trees look dead because all their leaves are gone, but Papa said the leaves will come back in the spring.

That's a sign of the spring. I know what it means now.

Uncle Frederick said he'd take us sledding at Hinckley Lake and for hot chocolate afterwards, when the real winter snow begins. Sledding means going down a snowy hill, faster, faster, faster, before shooting out onto the frozen lake. It sounds like fun, not at all like hurry, hurry, hurry. I want to invite the Kramers and The Tremont Rocket Club to Hinckley Lake for sledding.

After the first bell, I show Mrs. Washburn my sign:

I have a bird named Dog. I need newspapers for his eating, his sleeping, and his toileting. Dog is big. Please give many newspapers.

Mrs. Washburn asks, "Pete, why is your bird named Dog?"

I make a clucking sound.

"He's a rooster? So…why is your rooster named Dog?"

"He makes a sound, 'Bwarf.' Dog is Venezuelan, an araucana."

"An araucana? That's interesting. Are you asking the class for newspapers?"

"No. Papa at work will ask. I need better English than Papa has. May you help me?"

"I can help you."

Mrs. Washburn takes a small piece of poster board out of the art closet. She marks the margins and the lines in light pencil. Students run around the classroom but my teacher is not paying attention. She's focused on the poster.

She holds it up to me. "How's that?"

I have an araucana, rare rooster from South America named Dog. My family needs a lot of newspapers for Dog.

Could you please donate your daily newspaper? Could you donate as many other newspapers as you can?

Thank you very much,

the Buczkowskis.

"Thank you, Mrs. Washburn."

For the next two weeks, Papa staggers through the front door with piles of newspapers under each arm. People who work at the Cleveland City Club and people who eat there, too, all want to help.

And then one day, about a week before Christmas, Papa comes home with no newspapers and a big smile on his face.

"I've been in the club rooms, asking for extra newspapers for Dog. One of the members of The Cleveland City Club is an executive at the Zoo. I don't speak English, he doesn't speak Polish. We had to settle on German.

"In German, Mr. Rankin said the Cleveland Zoo would be happy to take Dog as the newest animal for their South American exhibit. Dog will live with South American plants and he'll eat South American food. The Zoo keeps the exhibit well heated, just like the Amazon River basin."

"Dog will live at the Cleveland Zoo?" Myron asks.

"He'll live in an exhibit that'll remind him of New Barcelona. He'll be happy there, happier than living here."

"When will we get to see him?" I ask.

"Mr. Rankin said he'd give us passes. We can go to the Zoo any time we want for free."

"Free?" Dog would be happier, a lot happier, at the Zoo.

"There's more news. Another club member is an editor of *The Cleveland Plain Dealer.* He wants to send a reporter and a photographer over here. He wants them to write an article--how did we come to live in Cleveland? How did Dog come to live here?"

I snap my fingers. "Papa, next week is Dog's first birthday. Remember? He was born on Christmas Eve. The Zoo could have a birthday party for him."

"What a wonderful idea."

"I could invite my class to the party."

"I'll invite my class, too," Myron says, "and my checkers club."

"Karol, I can't have my photograph taken, not in a twenty-five-old dress. I'll look like a refugee."

Papa turns to Mama. "Katrina, do you remember the department store we saw in Public Square? When we first came to Cleveland? Higbee's Department Store has dresses, and shoes, and handbags, but only if you'll get on the trolley to buy them."

"I can't do that."

"You just went to Uncle Frederick's for Thanksgiving," Myron reminds her.

"Dog would want you to wear a new dress for his birthday party," I say, which sounds ridiculous, but maybe it'll work.

"If we take the trolley together," Mama says faintly. "If Dog could come all the way to Cleveland, I can go to Higbee's. I'll need a dress and shoes."

“Let’s go tomorrow morning,” I say. “It’s Christmas vacation. No school.”

“Tomorrow morning?” Mama’s hands flutter to her chest.

Papa says, “The reporter wants to interview us as soon as possible.”

“I don’t have a coat to wear. It’s too cold. I can’t go.”

Myron reaches under the sofa and pulls out the last coat the Methodists gave us. It’s a woman’s coat of palest gray, like shadow on fresh snowfall.

Mama takes the coat in her arms. “This is a cashmere coat. Where did it come from?”

“The Methodists,” Papa says.

“Mama, look.” Zenon pulls long leather gloves out of the pockets. The gloves are just a shade darker than the coat.

“This must be a mistake. Nobody would give away such an elegant cashmere coat and gloves. We’ll have to give it back, Karol.”

“Boys, take Mama’s coat outside and give it a good shake. A good shake will smooth out the wrinkles and free the dust. We’ll take the trolley to Higbee’s tomorrow.”

“But—“

"Katrina, your sons need good clothes for the newspaper photograph, for Dog's birthday party. Think of it, our sons have never had new clothes."

Papa finds a seat in the back of the trolley. Mama, my brothers, and I sit in the front just behind the driver. Myron opens the window, to look at the electrical sparks once more, but the driver tells him to close it. It's too cold.

As the trolley lurches away from our apartment building, Mama grasps my right hand. She squeezes it hard.

The trolley runs on steel tracks. At every stop, the driver gets out and brushes the snow away from the front of the trolley.

"I'll be late for work," a passenger barks. "Can't it go faster?"

"We don't want snow reaching up to the windows," the driver answers. "The windshield wipers can only do so much."

"I'll be late for work," the passenger grumbles again.

Hurry, hurry, hurry….

"When I was a little girl, I had courage, Pedrito." Mama meets my eyes to make sure I'm listening.

"I'm listening."

"I rode my bicycle all over Warsaw, and out into the countryside. I knew how to ride a horse. I used to walk right up to strange dogs to pet them. I didn't know I had courage. I was…just…just me being me.

"Much later in the work camp, I realized that courage came from the absolute belief that my parents stood behind me. They were there to carry me, no matter what. I took risks I didn't know I was taking because they were there to pick me up if I ever fell down.

"After I lost everyone in my family, no one cared if I lived or died. That's when I lost my courage. We were visiting family in the countryside when the Nazis invaded. They took everyone in the district and sent them to the work camps. It didn't matter that my sisters and brothers and me, and my mother and father, were city people on a holiday. It didn't matter to them at all.

"My best girlfriend in Warsaw was taking care of our cat and our dog. I never saw them again. I never saw our house, my friends, my school, my classmates, and my teacher again.

"Oh, I had problems before I was a potato slave. I've never liked crowds of people. I've never liked going into strange buildings. But ever since the work camp, I've always felt like I was falling off a cliff, and it's too late, my heels are already in the air."

"What makes you happy, Mama?"

"Watching my boys grow up safely."

"President Thomas Jefferson said our freedoms come from God—life, liberty, and the pursuit of happiness."

Mama turns her face to the trolley window. "God and I parted company a long time ago."

"I'm just beginning to understand Him," I reply, "how He works in the world. I'm free to have courage because you and Papa are standing behind me, of course. But God is there too, an everlasting rock. We're so blessed. "

New clothes are itchy and stiff. I wear my new clothes for the photographer and the reporter from the *Cleveland Plain Dealer*, but as soon as they leave, my brothers and I take them off. Clothes worn by Methodists are much softer, and much more comfortable.

Papa brings the newspaper home from work. There are the Buczkowskis, sitting at the kitchen table with Dog standing right in the middle, next to the napkins. Dog is staring boldly, right into the camera.

Immigrant Family with Rare Rooster to Celebrate New Home at Cleveland Zoo

A rooster named Dog has come all the way from Venezuela to be re-united with his family, the Buczkowskis. The Buczkowskis immigrated to greater Cleveland on August 31st of this year.

"It's his birthday on the 24th," thirteen-year-old Pete Buczkowski, and owner of the rooster, said to this reporter. "Everyone in my class at Tremont Elementary School is invited to Dog's birthday party at the Zoo."

"Everyone in my class is invited, too," said Pete's brother, eight-year-old Myron, "I wish for chocolate cake and chocolate ice cream." Myron also attends Tremont Elementary.

When asked about the rooster's unusual name, Dog, the Buczkowskis laughed. They all said together, "Bwarf. Bwarf." Right on cue, the rooster barked like a dog. "Bwarf. Bwarf."

Mrs. and Mr. Buczkowskis are refugees from Poland, who were granted visas to come to the United States after living in Venezuela for more than ten years. "It was worth the wait," Mr. Buczkowski said as his sons translated. "To live in this country with all the opportunities for my sons are dreams come true."

Dog's birthday party will be held as a private party at the South American exhibit on Christmas Eve afternoon at two o'clock. Zoo patrons may see Dog on January 2nd, when the Cleveland Zoo re-opens after the holidays....

Mama is horrified at the photograph. "Everyone

will think we let a bird eat with us."

After breakfast, Mrs. Washburn stops by with extra copies of yesterday's *The Cleveland Plain Dealer.* She promises to let every student in class know about the party, "just in case their parents don't read the newspaper."

"How will you do this?" I ask.

My teacher makes a fist with her left hand and holds it next to her left ear. With her right hand, she twirls her index finger around and around.

She must have noticed my baffled stare. "I'll telephone everyone, Pete."

On December 24th, Uncle Frederick, Aunt Caroline, and the twins pick us up for the party. Most of my class comes to the party; most of Myron's class is there, too. There must be 100 people at Dog's birthday party.

There are massive sheets of chocolate cake and gallons of chocolate ice cream.

On the cakes is written:

Happy First Birthday, Dog!

There's icing paintings of Dog on the cakes, with bright orange, yellow, green, blue, and red frosting for his feathers and comb. Yellow frosting for his feet;

brown frosting for his tail feathers. The roosters are beautiful.

Mrs. Washburn tells me that I'll join the sixth grade reading class after the Christmas holiday. "If you need help, let me know. I'll give you extra homework."

"Lucky you, extra homework," Luis says, as the members of The Tremont Rocket Club laugh.

Myron runs by, his face smeared to the ears with chocolate cake and melted chocolate ice cream. "How much cake is that?" I ask.

"Chocolate twice a day," he says. "We can't fall behind."

"Says who?"

"Americans have chocolate twice a day."

"That's not true. You've had enough."

It seems peculiar, to have a conversation with Myron in English. But we've made a pact. We're going to speak only English with each other. That way, we'll learn it as fast as possible. Someday, Zenon will join our pact and we'll be like a typical American family—speaking English to one another. At least, the children in the family.

The same photographer and reporter from *The Cleveland Plain Dealer* are at the party, to write another article and take more photographs.

And Dog is here, of course. He's in the South American wing of the bird exhibit. He lives among South American plants, and his prey is South American cockroaches. We all cheer as he chases them fiercely around his new home.

There's a jungle trail of sorts and it winds around the perimeter of the exhibit. My brothers and I smile as we watch Dog run, his golden tail feathers bobbing between the broad leaves. He must be looking for bugs, pursuing happiness. Bwarf. Bwarf.

Day by day, Mama is better, stronger, for Dog has given her some of his bravery. He's shared with the Buczkowskis the fierce mettle Americans so admire. Anytime I feel my nerve flagging, my brand-new, spruce courage waning, we take the bus to the Zoo on Saturdays and Dog's self-assurance rubs off on all of us for another week. Sometimes Stuart and Bobby Kramer come with us. Dog is always happy to see us all, especially when I have a few shreds of newspaper for him to eat.

On the way home, we stop at the Honey Hut for coconut ice cream bars dipped in dark chocolate. Delicious.

The Tremont Rocket Club goes to Dennis's house on Friday afternoons to watch *The Adventures of*

Superman. Dennis's mother makes popcorn and we drink iced Pepsi-Colas. Here in America the Nazis do seem more like TV villains than evil *Niemskie Swinie.* We always cheer when one good Superman uppercut punch defeats them—pounded to smithereens—and after a word from our sponsors, stay tuned for a preview of next week's exciting *The Adventures of Superman.*

But Mama will always be broken in places that will never heal. And those places that do heal? They will forever have a scar. Dog and our family will help Mama all we can, but broken and scarred she'll stay.

As for me, I've always wanted everyone to be happy, but it's about the pursuit, isn't it? President Jefferson was right: No guarantees except the freedoms God has given us, the freedoms God has given to everyone.

Mrs. Washburn June 6th 1959

6th Grade Essay

Pete Buczkowski

How to Turn an Elevator into a Rocket

When I was first learning English, I tried to write a sentence about how an elevator becomes a

rocket. My sentence was too filled up with words, ideas, magic, pretending, hoping, wishing, and Cal Tech and MIT. I stopped trying to write this sentence.

Now that I've learned more English, I write paragraphs instead. Paragraphs are better because how to turn an elevator into a rocket is complicated, with much thinking and completing complex steps.

My family first came to America last August. It was my birthday. On the first day, we went into an elevator in the NYC hotel. My brothers and I felt stark terror in the elevator. The door shut and the tiny room went up, and up. The tiny room had no windows. Where were we going? What would happen once we got there? We felt much terror.

The next day, my youngest brother pretended this elevator was a rocket. He was no longer a fearful refugee. He was a fearless rocket man. That afternoon, my younger brother Myron and I went on top of the Empire State building. More than one hundred floors—the elevators went up, and up, and up, and up. We pretended to be fearless rocket men. We were no longer timid refugee boys from the jungle.

Is this pretending? Is this wishing? Is this hoping? Most people would say yes. We were just boys. As President Thomas Jefferson would say, we were chasing the happiness.

Most Americans would say no. Americans have technical schools like Cal Tech and MIT, and the teachers in the schools are helping the students learn to make rockets.

Americans are working hard to make rockets that will leave the Earth, leave the atmosphere, and go to the moon, the planets, and the stars.

Will people be on the moon someday? Most people would say no. Americans would say yes.

Most people would say, "Space journeys are just a dream."

Most Americans would say, "This is a dream that will come true because of science, math, hard work, and curiosity. We will work hard. It makes us happy to be curious, to expect the better; to pursue this dream will make us happy."

This is why Americans are different. This is how Americans will turn an elevator into a rocket.

Afterword

What happened to Pedrito, and his family and friends?

Ivan served hard time in a federal prison in Illinois.

Tolic is an international banker in Australia.

Stefan Bliatok recovered completely from his tropical illness. The Venezuelan government gave him a scholarship to attend medical school in Tulane University in New Orleans, Louisiana. He did research in tropical diseases for the Center for Disease Control in Atlanta, Georgia. When he retired, he returned to Venezuela and works as a clinic doctor in a poor section of Caracas.

Myron Buczkowski is in the security business.

Zenon Buczkowski died of a brain hemorrhage when he was a young man.

In 1947, Pedrito (Pete) Buczkowski was born in a Displaced Persons camp in post-war West Germany. In 1949, he and his parents immigrated to Venezuela where his brothers were born. The family immigrated to Cleveland, Ohio 11 years later. Pete is an honorably discharged Vietnam veteran and is partially disabled. He is a college graduate with degrees in Business and

Marketing. He speaks Spanish, English, Ukrainian, German, Polish, and Russian.

Mr. Buczkowski worked in marketing and as a civil engineer. He lives in a suburb of Akron, Ohio.

The Yanomani

The Yanomani do practice endocannibalism. After a close relative dies, his or her body is cremated. The bone ashes are eaten in rituals to remember the dead. Although they do kill rivals in battles, there is no evidence they eat the bones or flesh of anyone other than deceased family members.

Communism

In October 1917, Russia became the United Soviet Socialist Republic. It became a communist country. Their leaders killed millions of Russians, and other people in Eastern Europe nations, who didn't want to be communists. When Poland declared their independence from Communist Russia in 1989, other Eastern European nations quickly did the same. The communist regime ended in Russia in August 1991.

Simon Bolivar

Simon Bolivar was born in Caracas, Venezuela on July 24th, 1783. He helped liberate the nations of Venezuela, Columbia, Bolivia, Panama, Ecuador, and Peru from Spanish colonial control. He died on December 17th, 1830.

The Post-War World

There's an expression, "Don't put all your eggs in one basket." In the 30 years after WWII, the United States not only had all the eggs, we were the only nation holding a basket. In those years, the United States was a manufacturing empire, an export empire, a military empire, an agricultural empire, and a cultural empire. We were an economic colossus in a world full of poor nations.

At no time in world history did more people enjoy more wealth, more opportunity, and more security than did Americans after WWII.

Every novel is a collaboration and *Dog* is no exception. This author wishes to thank the South Carolina Writers Association, Surfside Beach Branch, for all their help, suggestions, and encouragement. I'd also like to thank Regina, Jocquelle, and Prathima for their unfailing enthusiasm and expertise.

The cover was painted by Diana Durrant, who is not only my niece, but a gifted artist.

And, this author wishes to thank Mike, who made it all possible.

Thank you for buying this novel. Please write a review about *Dog* on Amazon.com or Good Reads.

Other works by Lynda Durrant include:
Echohawk,
The Beaded Moccasins, the Story of Mary Campbell,
My Last Skirt, Jeanne Hodgers, Union Soldier,
Ariel Bradley, Spy for General Washington,
Imperfections
Betsy Zane, the Rose of Fort Henry

Made in the USA
Middletown, DE
18 May 2021

39109220R00136